# STU TRULY
## FIRST KISS

# STU TRULY

# TRULY

## FIRST KISS

### DAN RICHARDS

YELLOW JACKET

# YELLOW JACKET

An imprint of Little Bee Books, Inc.
251 Park Avenue South, New York, NY 10010
Text copyright © 2019 by Dan Richards
Jacket illustration by Simini Blocker
All rights reserved, including the right of reproduction
in whole or in part in any form.
Yellow Jacket is a trademark of Little Bee Books, Inc., and
associated colophon is a trademark of Little Bee Books, Inc.
Manufactured in the United States of America   LAK 0419
First Edition

10  9  8  7  6  5  4  3  2  1

Library of Congress Cataloging-in-Publication Data
is available upon request.
ISBN 978-1-4998-0891-9
yellowjacketreads.com

To the Tighty Writeys—
you know who you are.

Thanks for everything!

Truth is, I don't know much about girls. Not that I should. I'm only thirteen and I still keep a lightsaber tucked under my bed. Until recently, I was just a typical middle school kid without a care, or chin hair, in the world.

But sometimes life throws the unexpected at you. Like when a new girl comes prancing into your school and turns everything upside down. A girl unlike any girl you've ever known, who makes your mouth go dry, your words jumble up, and your thoughts go all wacky every time you see her. A girl who convinces you to do things, strange things you would never in a million years have done before, like agreeing to see *Unbounded Love,* the story of a soldier who loses his legs in the war, and the nurse who helps him learn to walk—and love—again.

"Don't they make a perfect couple?" Becca asked, leaning close.

I mean, I love going to the movies. But maybe I should have paid more attention to the title before agreeing to spend the first day of summer vacation trapped in a theater watching a war movie turn into a romantic pile of—

"Yeah, perfect," I lied.

Ben leaned close on my other side. He wiggled his butt until a wet, squelchy sound shook my seat.

"Here's what I call—"

He scooched again. Another squishy sound gurgled up.

"—a perfect couple!"

I should explain that Sequim, pronounced like "squid" but with an *m* at the end, is too small to have a real theater. Our only movie house is a converted Presbyterian church located next door to the library. The seats came from some famous turn-of-the-century theater that was being torn down in Seattle. They're so old they still have real leather covers with real metal springs that make real intestinal noises—if you know how to slide around just right. Ben's an expert.

The two ladies seated in front of him turned with looks of disapproval. Kirsten punched his arm.

"You're disgusting," she whispered with a giggle. She slid back in her seat until a curdled hiss seeped out from beneath her.

Ben and I doubled over. Sometimes Kirsten was better at being Ben than Ben, especially when it came to intestinal noises.

I sat back up just in time to catch the climactic moment of the movie. The two main characters were locked in an embrace, their lips pressed together in an act of undying love.

Something primal stirred at the thought of Becca sitting only an armrest away. I glanced over. The curve of her lips perfectly matched the heroine's lips on-screen. The zombie warlord in my chest immediately woke up and pounded out a message in Morse code on my ribs: R-U-N W-H-I-L-E Y-O-U S-T-I-L-L C-A-N.

I agreed wholeheartedly. If only my feet were

listening. As usual, they were sleeping peacefully at the end of each slumbering leg, blissfully unaware of the danger looming above. I reached for my kneecap to slap some sense into it, but instead my hand brushed against Becca's. It froze there as if held by some magnetic force. Ben's fist bumped my leg. I looked over to find him grinning.

"You the man," he whispered.

Easy for him to say. Kirsten's hand had been locked in his since the movie started. Seeing them that way made my stomach churn. Shouldn't we be doing something more productive right now? Like finishing level thirty-three of *Death Intruders 4*? Personally, I'd rather face a ravenous army of the undead than sit here trying to stop my hand from fluctuating between arctic cold and Saharan sweaty.

At last, the movie ended. Becca's knuckles slipped away from mine as we got up to leave. I let out a breath. I'm not saying I didn't like the electric charge of my hand being so close to hers. I'm just saying next time I needed more warning so I could steady my nerves or at least slather my hands with antiperspirant.

We exited into the warm afternoon. My hand still tingled from where her skin had been in contact. Things were happening too fast. I needed to go home and think things over. Maybe if I could slow it all down I could make sense of how a guy could be lured to see a war movie and, instead, end up almost holding hands during a kissing scene.

"Let's go get ice cream," Kirsten suggested.

"Yeah," Ben and Becca agreed.

So much for thinking things over.

**2**

It was a short walk to the ice cream parlor, just long enough for Ben to pull me aside.

"Dude, you and Becca are getting serious."

"Shut up."

He bumped my shoulder. "No, for real. You know what comes next after holding hands?"

Technically, we hadn't held hands. And anyway, of course I knew what came next: a long period of staying as far apart as possible. Far enough to figure out what was going on and how to make it stop. That would probably mean moving. Maybe overseas.

"Shut up."

Ben eyed me closely. "You don't know, do you?"

He seemed to be trying to make a point, but not one I wanted to hear. The short walk suddenly seemed impossibly long. At the rate we were going, he'd make sense before we got there.

He leaned close. "You're going to kiss," he whispered.

A bead of sweat ran down my forehead. In fact, I think my face literally melted and dribbled into the gutter.

"Shut up!" I said for the third time. I was beginning to wonder if those were the only words I knew. Around Ben they seemed to be all I needed.

"Seriously," he continued. "That's the way it works. You start going out, you hold hands, and then you kiss. I figure Kirsten and I got one or two weeks max before it's going to happen."

Ben's voice rose with the same excitement it always did when sharing a bit of news bound to make me retch. Usually it involved something he had read in *Ripley's Believe It or Not!*, like the guy who had two heads that were always finishing each other's sentences. But this was going too far. I could feel the words snaking inside my skull like a boa constrictor slowly squeezing my brain to death.

"You don't know what you're talking about."

He gave his best conspiratorial grin. "You'll see."

We followed the girls into the ice cream shop. The sweet smell was enough to temporarily distract me from Ben's words.

"I love bubble-gum ice cream," Kirsten bubbled.

"Ooh, with licorice gumdrops," Ben bubbled, too.

Becca stuck out her tongue. "Yuck. You like licorice gumdrops?"

"He loves anything that makes others want to vomit," I explained.

Ben nodded eagerly. "I'm all about the puking."

Kirsten rolled her eyes like the expert eye roller she had become. "Don't listen to him," she said to Becca. "He's just being Ben."

That girl seemed custom-made in heaven for that boy. Who else could ignore his puking jokes while licking bubble-gum ice cream? Not even I could pull that off, and I'd been best friends with him my whole life.

We slumped down at a table in the corner. Kirsten stabbed at her bubble-gum ice cream with a spoon. Ben slurped rainbow sherbet out of a cone. Becca nibbled at the marshmallows in her scoop of rocky road. And I attempted to inhale a mountain of chocolate chocolate-chip in a single bite.

"You must like chocolate," Becca observed.

"Yep," I agreed. "Ben's all about the puking, and I'm all about the chocolate."

"I'd rather be you," Becca said.

"Wouldn't everyone?" I agreed.

Ben took a massive slurp of sherbet. "Boring."

"True," I had to agree. "If puking's your thing."

Kirsten turned to Becca. "Isn't boy talk fun?"

Ben leaned across the table, a dribble of sherbet running down his chin. "Is it the puke talk? We can talk about something else, like embalming fluids. I once read that the Egyptians kept a dead pharaoh's fluids in a coffee mug so he could drink them for breakfast when he got to the afterlife."

"Pretty sure you're making that up," Becca said. She licked a chocolaty drip before it escaped from the bottom of her cone. "But I learned at my old school that they used to embalm the pharaoh's organs and

9

store them in clay jars next to the sarcophagus, and sometimes even put them back in the pharaoh's body before wrapping it."

Ben's jaw dropped, which unfortunately revealed a large glob of sherbet still in his mouth. "No way," he sputtered. "That's so cool. I have to look that up."

Kirsten pushed her bowl away and leaned back. "I hope our grades don't come in the mail today. I got an A-minus in both history and math."

"No, not *two* A-minuses," Ben said, slapping his hands to his cheeks in horror. "I'm with stupid," he quipped, motioning his head in her direction.

Kirsten and Becca froze. Neither spoke for what seemed like minutes. The social temperature dropped from warm banter to ice-cold awkwardness.

Abruptly, Kirsten got up. "I gotta get home."

"Me too," Becca whispered. She tried to give me a parting smile, but her mouth seemed permanently locked in an O shape.

The door to the shop banged shut, and Ben and I were left sitting alone.

"Want anything else?" the teenage girl behind the counter asked, oblivious to the sudden chill in the room.

Ben stared at the door like a lost puppy. "What happened? I was just kidding."

My mind whirled, trying to replay the last few moments. The mood had changed from teasing to sinister in seconds. Something had gone horribly wrong, but I couldn't quite put a finger on what. Did Kirsten really care that much about her grades? "I don't know." And I was pretty sure neither of us was going to figure it out.

I arrived home to find my mother waiting for me in the kitchen. Her face was all scrunched up like a whole sandwich that's been squeezed into a single sandwich bag.

"Stu," she began. "There's something I need to tell you—"

"Grandma fell and is going to die," my little brother, Tommy, announced as he ran into the room holding a toy plane in one hand while wielding a plastic sword in the other.

"Wh-what?" I stammered.

My mother directed him back into the living room. "I didn't say she was going to die. I said you are going to be the death of me if you don't get your shoes on."

She turned back to me. "Your grandmother fell this morning and broke her hip. Your father's already at the hospital. I've been waiting for you to get home so we can go meet him there."

It's important to note my grandmother is not exactly my grandmother. She married my grandfather after his first wife died. That made her my dad's stepmother and my step-grandmother. My grandfather passed away a couple years ago, so technically speaking, we're not really related other than sharing the same last name. But since she gives me money every year for my birthday, I don't quibble over the details. Oh, and she can do card tricks like a real magician, which pretty much makes her the coolest grandma ever.

"Is she okay?"

My mother jammed a couple bags of raisins and a box of animal crackers into her purse, then dragged my little brother, wearing only one shoe, out the door to the car.

"Your father called a few minutes ago and said the doctors are discussing options with her right now." She buckled my brother into his seat, then ran back inside and returned with his other shoe. "Put this on him while I drive," she said, handing me the shoe.

So much for riding shotgun. I climbed into the back seat and went to work. Trying to get a shoe on my little brother was like trying to shoe a wild horse. He kicked every time the sneaker came near his foot.

"Stop kicking," I commanded.

That only enraged his My-Angry-Little-Pony act further.

"I can do it myself!" Tommy yelled.

"Then why don't you?" I yelled back, tossing the shoe at him.

I slouched against the window. First, I accidentally almost held hands with Becca, then Kirsten walked out on Ben, and now I find out my grandmother broke her hip. Pretty sure the day couldn't get any weirder.

The only hospital nearby is in Port Angeles, about fifteen miles away. That meant twenty minutes of watching my brother twist, pull, and impale himself with his own shoe. Apparently five is the age when a kid discovers that if you kick like a mule while putting on your sneaker, you get a black eye in return.

"Ow!" my brother cried, grabbing at his eye.

"What did you do to your brother?"

My mother had a terrible habit of assuming things.

"He kicked himself in the eye," I said calmly.

"Stu," my mother baited me.

"Seriously, he kicked himself in the eye."

She glanced back at Tommy in the rearview mirror. "Don't kick yourself in the eye," she scolded Tommy.

"I don't like it," Tommy shouted. He threw his shoe into the front passenger seat.

"Please help your brother," my mother said, handing me back the shoe.

And so round two of shoeing My-Angry-Little-Pony began. This time I got the upper hand by squeezing his leg between my arm and rib cage to hold it steady.

"Ow!"

"Just hold still for a moment."

"Ow!"

*Seriously?* I was the one getting the chipotle kicked out of me.

I finally managed to jam his foot into the shoe and

tie the laces like the expert calf roper I had become. His shod leg dropped limp and sneakered, and I returned to my slouching spot against the window. Whoever decided children should wear shoes obviously didn't have a little brother.

A few minutes later, we passed a sign that read WELCOME TO PORT ANGELES. My father liked to say Sequim is a good place to die, but Port Angeles is the best place to get a job. The city was built next to the Strait of Juan de Fuca, a waterway that runs between the US and Canada. It has a ferry that takes passengers across the strait to Victoria, British Columbia, and a port that ships lumber all the way to Asia. People retire in Port Angeles, too, but you almost don't notice them unless you're looking—unlike in Sequim, where it seems like everyone is one final breath from the afterlife.

We turned off the main road and wound our way through streets of little houses before reaching a narrow parking lot with a view of the strait. The hospital stood on a bluff high above the water, much like the hospital Ben and I visited on level twenty-seven of

16

*Death Intruders 3*, except the power had been cut to that hospital and zombies were roaming the halls. In comparison, this hospital looked pretty normal, like someone might actually want to be sick there.

My mother hurried us inside and up an elevator to the third floor. A big desk area with nurses behind computers took up the middle part of the floor, surrounded by rows of patient rooms on either side. I tried to ignore the antiseptic smell, and the churning feeling in my stomach. Being around sick people made me feel, well . . . sick.

All the more reason not to peek into the rooms as we passed, but I couldn't help it. What I saw looked right out of *Death Intruders*. Pale, sickly people in hospital gowns lying in shiny metal beds hooked up to all sorts of computer monitors and bottles of dripping fluids. All that was missing were chain saws, flamethrowers, and a couple dozen zombies roaming about to make the horror complete.

We reached room 318, and my mother ushered us inside. Behind a sliding curtain, my grandmother lay in bed, my father sitting next to her. I guess I expected her to look all pale and unconscious like the other patients we had passed, but instead, she seemed as fiery as ever.

"No need for all the fuss," she told my mother. "I'm doing fine."

"She needs surgery," my father added. "They're working out the details now, but it will probably be tomorrow morning."

"I don't need surgery," my grandmother said. "I'm fine."

My father patted her hand. "She's on pain meds. Don't believe anything she says."

My mother took her other hand. "We're right here and will make sure the doctors take good care of you."

"I'm fine," my grandmother said again. She tried to sit up and let out a groan. "Well, maybe not entirely fine, but I don't need surgery."

She eased back against a pillow and pressed a button that sent a drip into the IV tube connected to her arm.

"You're gonna have to trust the doctors," my father said in a soothing voice. "They know what they're doing."

"Since when do doctors know anything?" she asked, her speech starting to slur.

"Since you fell this morning and broke your hip in two places," he replied.

Her eyes looked dreamy. "But what about the store? I can't take time off to heal from some blasted surgery."

My grandmother owns Truly Fine Fashions, the only women's clothing store in Sequim. According to my mom, it's a real pillar of the community.

"I'm afraid you are going to be housebound for a few weeks after the surgery," my father explained so gently it sounded like she was about to depart on a tropical vacation. "The store will have to survive without you for a little while."

"That's impossible," she argued. "My customers need me."

She winced and pressed the button again. Another drip slid down her IV.

"They'll still need you when you return," my father countered.

Her eyes drooped until she looked to be half asleep. "But Elsa needs help," she slurred. "I can't afford another Elsa."

Elsa was my grandmother's only employee at the

store. I met her one time when my mother dragged me in looking for some truly fine sundries, whatever those are.

"Don't you worry," my father crooned. "We'll find someone to help out until you're all healed."

"I've got the perfect person in mind," my mother added, all too excitedly. "Someone with all the time in the world until school starts again."

She grabbed my hand and pulled me to the bedside.

"Stu!"

That led to a lively discussion that evening.

"I am *not* working at her store!" I said for the umpteenth time.

"The decision isn't yours to make," my mother countered for the umpteenth time. "Family helps family. That's the way it works around here."

Yeah, that's where it usually goes wrong. The last time I helped family, it ended up with me wearing a rack of ribs costume in front of thousands of people at the Irrigation Festival Parade. That was less than two months ago. How could I be asked to help family again so soon?

"It's not fair," I whined, stealing a line from my little brother.

My father uncrossed his arms long enough to let out a heavy sigh.

"Life isn't fair," he explained. "But think of it this way, your grandmother has been giving you money on special occasions all these years, and this is your chance to repay her."

Hang on a minute. No one ever told me holiday gifts were loans that had to be repaid. It put a whole new spin on the holidays, and I didn't like the implications. If birthdays were putting me deeply in debt, how was I supposed to pay for college? Or a new game controller?

"Don't worry," my mother said. "I've been in touch with Elsa. She only needs help at the store between ten and two each day. That will leave plenty of time for you to lounge about the house and hang out with your friends."

My mother didn't seem to understand that the prime lounging hours were between ten and two. Also, before ten and after two, but now was not the time to bring that up.

"Do I still have to do my chores?" Being a shrewd negotiator, I saw an opportunity to sweeten the deal.

"When did you start doing your chores?" my father asked.

My mother muffled a laugh. "Yes, you will still need to do your chores, preferably without being asked."

So much for negotiating.

"When do I have to start?"

"Tomorrow," my father replied.

That gave me one whole evening of freedom before I became a working dog for the rest of my life and probably the afterlife, too. I slumped out of the living room and hurried over to Ben's house for some much-needed guy time.

# 5

"I ordered pizza," he said, ushering me into the family room. "My parents should know better than to leave petty cash lying around." He handed me a can of Orange Splash. "Or sugary sodas."

"Don't worry, the soda is healthy," I said, pointing to the label. It read *Calcium and vitamin C injected into every can.*

"Good point," Ben agreed. "That offsets the tooth decay and diabetes. We better have two."

We spent the rest of the evening enjoying our new favorite pastime: zombie football. After finishing level thirty-two of *Death Intruders 4*, several bonus games had been unlocked. Our favorite was zombie football. It was just like real football, except with chain saws and zombies. With practice, Ben and I had learned how to carry a football and a chain saw at the same time. The key was to remember which one was in your throwing hand before making a pass.

"How many times you gonna do that?" Ben asked, picking his receiver's head up off the ground, an errantly thrown chain saw lying nearby in the grass.

"Sorry," I apologized. "I'm distracted. My grandma's in the hospital, and my parents are making me work at her store starting tomorrow."

Ben made a choking sound. "You mean like a real job?"

"Kinda, but I'm not getting paid."

"What? That's crazy! There are child labor laws against that sort of thing. Did you show them your armpits? Clearly, you're still a child."

With that sort of eloquence, Ben had a future arguing cases in court. Or at least having his head used as a gavel.

"I don't think those laws apply when your grandma has a broken hip."

"Dude, that stinks."

"You got that right." Not even pizza could take the

sting out of what I was being forced to do. I had two more slices just to prove my point. After popping open my second soda, I broached the other question on my mind.

"You talk to Kirsten since earlier?"

Ben swallowed a massive bite of cheese and took a swig from his soda, then crushed the can with one hand. "Nope."

That pretty much ended that topic. Further discussion would have meant contemplating things neither of us knew anything about or wanted to consider. An hour later, gut stuffed, sugar buzz crashing, and thumbs numb from hours of zombie football, I reached the simple conclusion that it was time to head home.

"Don't let your grandma down tomorrow, young man," Ben said at the door with a parting wave. "Those pantsuits won't sell themselves."

If only they made a pantsuit large enough to bag that boy's head. "Shut up."

I headed home while massaging circulation back into my thumbs. Football really is a contact sport.

My thumbs might actually need an ice bath when I got home.

Near the corner, I paused to stare up at Becca's house. Since things had ended a bit awkwardly earlier, the prudent thing would be to pop in, pull her onto the porch, apologize for my friend's brutish behavior, and give her a polite kiss good night.

Say what? The thought made my hands tremble, and toxic beads of sweat began dripping from my pits. How could I let such a thought bully its way into my mind? I shoved it to the side to make room for another, more urgent thought. Was there such a thing as a kissing phobia? If so, I had a severe case. I was probably the first boy to ever go out with a girl and not want to—

Wait a minute! Since when were Becca and I going out? Yes, we'd hung out a few times. And today there may have been a few minutes when our knuckles touched. But that didn't mean we were going out, did it? And even if it did, we were a long way from our lips ever touching. Weren't we?

Ben! It was all Ben's fault for bringing up the idea. He had made me believe that handholding automatically led to kissing. But the only thing his fat lips had ever kissed was an ice-cold metal fence post in second grade. I knew how that had ended. He's lucky he still has lips.

He couldn't possibly know what he was talking about. Right?

Ten o'clock the next morning came way too soon. I found myself standing at the front door of my grandmother's store.

"Stu, it's time to go in," my mother said.

Easy for her to say. She wasn't the one being sent to a labor camp. I glanced around to make sure none of my friends were watching. Main Street at this ungodly hour was pretty much empty, except for two ladies heading our way.

"Hi, Molly," one of the ladies greeted my mother.

"Hi, Judy," my mother replied.

The other woman gave her a hug.

"We heard about Rosemarie's fall," she said. "Such a shame. I hope she's better soon. We're all going to miss her dearly at the store."

"Yes," my mother said. "I keep hearing that. They did surgery first thing this morning. The doctor said it went well and they expect a full recovery."

"Oh, that's marvelous!" Judy responded. "We're planning to stop by the hospital and see her later today."

"I'm sure she'd appreciate that," my mother said, pushing me toward the door. "For the moment, I need to take Rosemarie's replacement inside so Elsa can show him around."

I tried to smile but stopped short. They were eyeing me like a rodent who had just crawled out of the sewer.

"Oh," Judy said. "That's . . . nice."

"He's excited to help out," my mother lied.

The other woman put her hand over her heart, either to check her pulse or to ward off evil spirits.

"I see," she muttered. "I'm sure he'll . . . be . . . just . . ." Her voice trailed off.

I knew exactly how she felt. Though I would have preferred if she'd been less obvious in stating the obvious. A thirteen-year-old boy had to be the last person that women wanted working in a women's clothing store. If only my mother had listened when I explained that to her. It might have helped if I had been less hysterical at the time.

I tucked my rodent tail between my legs and shuffled inside. Neither of the ladies followed. Their shopping needs had apparently changed. Strange, they had seemed so excited moments before.

The interior of the store was a spectacle of clothing, shoes, and accessories displayed on shelves, carts, tables, wall hooks, and circular racks, with mirrors conveniently placed pretty much everywhere. The smell of flower-laced perfume hung in the air. I'd been to the carnival lots of times but had never seen a house of horrors this frightening. All it needed was a ghostly soundtrack to complete the effect.

Elsa hurried over to where I stood gaping.

"Stu!" she cried. "I'm so happy to have your help."

"Yeah," I squeezed out. "Happy."

She ushered me to the back room, where a bunch of unopened boxes had been tossed in a pile.

"Look what arrived today. Fall fashions!" She beamed as if the boxes were full of treasure. "I've worked here almost twelve years and I still get excited to see the latest inventory!" She looked at me as if expecting me to share her enthusiasm.

"Great," I lied. "Can't wait."

She took me by the arm and proceeded to show me around the store. From her glowing descriptions, the place was a wonderland of beauty, art, and sophistication. I wasn't exactly sure what *sophistication* meant, but I'm pretty sure it didn't mean cool, fun, or free pizza.

"If you don't mind working in the back room, I was hoping you could get all the boxes opened while I stay out here to greet customers. There's a box cutter on the top shelf."

Would I mind staying out of sight in the back? Seriously? The only thing better would be a secret door in the floor that led to a safe room underground. "Sure. That sounds fine."

I found the box cutter and plopped myself down on the nearest box. After doing a little math, I calculated if I opened one box every fifteen minutes it would take exactly four hours to finish. Cutting tape that slowly wouldn't be easy, but I was willing to man up and meet the challenge.

An hour later, I was bored out of my mind but right on schedule. My father always says a man should take pride in his work. Amen. My chest puffed out at the realization that not just any man could slice tape at snail speed. But I wasn't just any man. I rubbed my smooth chin. Nope, I wasn't a man at all. If I were a man I wouldn't have been roped into this nightmare.

At least no one but Ben knew.

"Trying on a few things?"

I whirled to find Tyler and Ryan, my two closest friends other than Ben, grinning in the doorway.

"What are you doing here?" I asked.

"We called Ben to see if you guys wanted to hang out," Ryan explained.

"He told us you're into women's clothes now," Tyler added.

"Shut up. My grandma broke her hip, and I have to help out until she's better."

"Of course," Tyler agreed.

"But we know why you're *really* here," Ryan added. "To meet the ladies."

Tyler high-fived Ryan.

"Shut up."

Their giggling went on for far too long.

"Hey, can you cut out early?" Ryan asked. "Ben wants to have a zombie football tournament."

Tyler took the box cutter and tore open one of the boxes. "He talks like zombie football is the best thing ever."

I scooted over to keep my leg from being mistaken for a piece of tape. "It's a blast. But I'll have to meet you there after I get off work."

"Seriously?" Tyler lamented. "How long you gonna be working here?"

"Probably till I die. Or at least until summer's over." Both sounded equally depressing. "Hey, why weren't you guys at the movie yesterday?"

The silly grins on their faces drooped.

"Gretchen and I broke up," Ryan explained.

Huh? "You had been going out?" I asked.

A slow burn crept up his cheeks.

"About a week."

"Annie broke up with me, too," Tyler interjected. "Girls are the worst."

"We're better off without them," Ryan said half-heartedly.

"Yeah," I agreed. "Who needs 'em?"

"What about you?" Tyler asked. "You still going out with Becca?"

Not them, too. Did my friends think Becca and I were going out? It's one thing to wonder that in secret, but why was the whole world jumping to that conclusion?

"We're not really going out," I offered. "We're just friends."

"Yeah, right," Ryan said. "You probably held her hand at the movie."

A flush crawled up my face that would soon eclipse the one on Ryan's. This conversation had gone far enough. What fool had even started it? Oops, my bad.

Tyler handed me back the box cutter and pushed Ryan out of the workroom.

"You better get going on those boxes if you ever want to get off work."

"Yeah, see ya later," Ryan added on their way out.

"Yeah, see you."

The clock finally struck 2:00 p.m. just as the last piece of tape split open on the last box. Funny how that had worked out. I stumbled out of the workroom and headed for the front door, wondering how much the world had changed. It felt like years had passed.

Before I got to the door, Elsa waved me over.

"Stu," she said. "I want you to meet Diane, one of our most loyal customers."

A heavyset woman with dyed black hair and bright red lipstick grinned at me. "So, you're Rosemarie's grandson?" She held out her hand. "Nice to meet you."

Her hand swallowed mine. I didn't know a woman could have hands that large. "N-nice to m-meet you," I stammered.

"I'm so sorry to hear about your grandmother," she continued, her voice choking. "She's meant a lot to me over the years. Don't know what I'd do without her."

I nodded.

She dabbed at one eye. "But we've got to be strong. That's the best way to show how much we care." She gave me a wink. "That and a bottle of wine."

Both ladies broke into giggles. I tried to smile, but

mostly I just stood there feeling out of place.

"As long as the fall fashion show still happens, everything will be okay," Diane said, fanning her face with one hand.

Elsa pulled a sky-blue blouse off the nearest rack and handed it to her. "Of course," she said. "Right, Stu?"

"The what?"

"The fall fashion show," Elsa explained. "It's the store's most important marketing event heading into the holidays. Every August since forever the store has hosted a fashion show to introduce the latest fall and winter fashions. All the ladies in town come."

"It's the event of the season," Diane added. "I wouldn't miss it for the world!"

Elsa handed Diane a pair of sky-blue stretch pants that matched the blouse. "Don't you worry. With Stu's help, we'll put on the best show yet."

Diane gave me a way-too-pleased smile. "Sounds like you're quite the fashionista, just like your grandmother."

Huh?

I left the store and inhaled the fresh air of freedom. The horrors of womanly clothing, womanly under-garments, and womanly perfume faded as I strolled through downtown. By downtown, I mean the lone street that contains the town's shops, including my grandmother's clothing store. The only time our down-town seems impressive is during the Irrigation Festival Parade, when thousands of people line the street. In reality, Sequim is like a hole in one of my gym socks, big enough to cause a blister, but not big enough to get me out of running laps in PE.

At the next light, I hung a right and left the downtown area. After passing block after block of little homes, I turned onto Ben's street and stopped short. Becca sat at the base of her steps with her arms curled around her legs, rocking slowly back and forth. Even from a distance, I could tell something was wrong.

"Hey, Becca."

"Hi," she replied through gritted teeth.

She scooted over, and I plunked down next to her.

"You okay?"

She returned to rocking. "My little sister is the worst! She always gets her way—even when she's being a total brat."

I could relate to that. "Yeah, my little brother's like that, too. Drives me crazy."

"My parents are making me switch rooms with her. She says she always gets the smaller room and it should be her turn to have the bigger room."

To be honest, if my room were the size of a shoebox, I wouldn't even notice. But now was not the time to bring that up. "That seems unfair. Once it's your room, it's your room."

She looked up, her eyes all fiery like the day she proposed the cafeteria sit-in to demand vegetarian entrée options be added to the school lunch menu.

"That's what I said. You can't make me move out of

my room! It's *my* room! But my mom got all preachy about fairness and stuff, and how I need to learn to think about others."

She looked ready to either cry or cuss. I prayed for a swearing fit. Foul language relaxes me, unlike crying. Crying makes me nervous, especially if it involves actual tears.

"It's not fair," she continued, a tear slipping down her cheek. "I have my room set up just the way I want. Everything is going to get ruined!"

I'm sure her words were important, but all I could focus on was the tear slowly working its way down her cheekbone to the edge of her chin. I prayed it was a lone rebel, and not the beginning of a flash flood. I could stare a zombie down without flinching, but I had no idea how to deal with the terror of a girl crying on her front steps.

"Maybe you could give her away on Craigslist," I tried. "I hear people will take anything you post for free."

That brought a giggle. "That's it. I'll give her away

to a family looking for a little brat to boss them around. Should be easy to find, right?"

She brushed the tear away. My body relaxed.

"Hey, I'll throw in my little brother, if it helps. Who can resist the offer of two free, whining little kids looking for a good home? It doesn't even need to be a good home. Any home will do."

Her giggle was followed by a snort. "I'll even throw in my parents to sweeten the deal."

"Wow, that's quite an offer. Who could refuse two free annoying children and two free annoying parents? I might take you up on that myself."

She smiled and wiped her other eye.

"So, what have you been up to?" she asked.

What had I been up to? Other than spending the day staring at boxes of women's clothing?

"Not much, just sleeping in and hanging around the house."

That might not have been entirely accurate, but I wasn't ready to share the news that I now worked in a women's clothing store. That place made me feel about as manly as having saggy biceps and downy-soft arm hair. There was a reason I kept my arms covered in public.

"Oh, that sounds pretty rough."

If only she knew.

"Yeah, living a life of leisure is hard, but someone has to do it."

She uncurled and stood. "Thanks for listening. I feel a little better. Guess I better get packing for the big move down the hall before my parents start cranking at me again."

"Maybe there's a cupboard under the stairs like in *Harry Potter* you can move into. That'd show 'em."

She flashed a smile. "Maybe."

"Never underestimate the power of guilt."

"Oh, I won't." She started back up the stairs, then stopped again. "Hey, are you doing anything next Sunday? My family is going to Lake Crescent for a picnic. Want to come?"

The thought of spending the day with Becca's family should have thrown up a warning flag. Not that I would have noticed. I'm not the kind of guy who pays attention to warning flags until it's way too late. "Sure, sounds like fun."

"Cool. See you then!"

Yeah, cool . . . right?

8

Something seemed off when I got to Ben's door. His house was strangely quiet. When Ryan and Tyler came over it was never quiet, there should've been laughter, or at least shouting. The hairs on the back of my neck prickled. Something was up, probably sinister.

My fears were confirmed when Ben's mother answered the door.

"I'm sorry Ben didn't let you know," she said. "His father needed him at the store. Maybe the two of you can hang out after he gets off work."

Ben's father owns Sequim Valley Hardware, a fine store carrying a wide variety of tools, household items, and gardening equipment. When I was little, I loved visiting the store because his dad kept one full aisle of toys. And not just any toys, Hot Wheels cars, toy shovels, toy tool sets, and best of all: toy commando gear. When you're eight years old, nothing grabs your attention like a commando utility belt complete with plastic radio, plastic ammo pockets, and real plastic grenades that make exploding sounds when they hit the ground. We were banned from touching the grenades after Ben and I ambushed a customer in the gardening aisle. We're still not allowed near the ornamental bird feeders.

The idea of Ben laboring in his father's sweatshop brought a certain devilish glee. Picturing his stubby little hands restocking shelves almost made my morning bearable. Rather than heading home, I sauntered back downtown. After all, the only thing better than gloating behind your best friend's back is gloating to his face.

~

"Looking for Ben?" his father asked, slipping a plastic grenade from my hand.

Funny. Somehow I had ended up in the toy aisle.

"I heard he was helping out today."

Ben's father led the way to the storeroom. "Oh, not

just today. Ben's going to be working here part-time from now on."

My smirk widened.

Near the back of the storeroom, I found Ben sweeping the floor. Or at least holding a broom used for sweeping.

"I think you missed a spot," I commented, pointing to the pile of dust I had just kicked up.

"Shut up."

"At least you're getting paid."

He gave me a look that could have melted metal.

"Aren't you?" I asked.

With a flick, his broom sent the pile of dust scattering in all directions.

"My parents saw my final grades this morning. They seem to think I'm not putting enough effort into school and need to learn the meaning of work."

Having witnessed Ben's work ethic at school, I could see their point.

"My dad says he'll start paying me when my grades get up to a B average."

"Wow, that could take years."

"Shut up. They're concerned if I don't get my grades up now I'll do the same thing in high school and not go to college."

"That's unfair—middle school grades don't count for high school."

He began sweeping the dust he had just scattered. "That's what I said. I'm just saving myself for when it really counts."

"They didn't believe you?"

"No. They think the habits you build when you're young carry over as you get older."

"What kind of crazy logic is that?"

"Exactly."

"So, what are you going to do?"

"What can I do? I'm going to sweep this floor every day until I die." He gave me a grin. "It's not all bad. At least I'm not selling undies to old ladies."

"Shut up." Clearly it was time to go.

⁓

At dinner that night, my mother asked a loaded question. "How was work today?"

Did she really want an answer? "Terrible, I work in a women's clothing store."

"Did Elsa show you the ropes?" my father asked.

"I guess." Only one customer had even come in while I was there. "I don't know. Mostly, I opened boxes in the back room."

My father nodded approval. "That's honest work you're doing. Pay attention and do as you're asked and you might just learn more than you expect."

That wouldn't take much since I wasn't expecting to learn anything.

"Your grandmother is doing well," my mother said. "They're going to keep her at the hospital for a couple more days and then she'll be moved to a nursing facility for a couple weeks until she's strong enough to go home." She leaned in. "What you are doing in helping Elsa is important. I hope you understand that."

The sincerity of her words wormed their way inside. She was right. I was doing something important. Something to be proud about.

The phone rang, and my mother went to answer it.

"Stu," she called. "It's for you."

"Hi, Stu," Elsa bubbled from the other end of the line. "I almost forget to tell you we're celebrating the color pink this week. Don't forget to wear pink tomorrow."

So much for my pride.

9

I arrived at the store the next morning sporting the pink polo shirt my mother scrounged from the hospital thrift store for me on my way to work. Yeah, it was a size too large, and entirely pink, including horizontal pink stripes, three pink buttons, and a pink alligator on the breast that looked like a prank intended to embarrass alligators everywhere.

"You look perfect!" Elsa exclaimed.

Yeah, a perfect idiot. "Thanks. Just trying to do my part."

"We're going to have fun this week," she continued. "You can help me decorate for our theme, Pretty in Pink. Everyone feels pretty in pink, you know."

Not everyone. I, for one, felt foolish in pink. But Elsa didn't seem the least bit interested in hearing that. She immediately handed me a roll of pink crepe paper and pointed to a ladder in the front window.

"I thought we could decorate the store like a high school prom with pink streamers and sprinkle pink confetti on all the tables."

Any interest I'd ever had about going to high school prom got tossed. By noon, the store fairly sparkled with pretty pinkness. Elsa stared around in wonder.

"It's so beautiful! Like right out of a storybook."

What sort of storybooks did she read? To me, it looked like the sugar-spun insides of a carnival cotton candy machine.

"Now we just need customers!" she enthused.

As if on cue, the door opened, and two women entered. When I say women, I mean two girls. And when I say two girls, I mean Becca and Kirsten.

The zombie warlord pounded on my chest reminding me I was dressed like a pink-polo-shirted dork.

"Lookin' good," Kirsten observed with a grin too wide to be believable.

"What are you guys doing here?" I asked.

"News travels quick," Becca said, grinning.

I should've known my guy friends couldn't keep a secret.

"Hello," Elsa said, holding out her hand in greeting. "I'm Elsa. Looks like you already know Stu."

Becca shook her hand. "Yes, we go to school together."

She and Kirsten exchanged conspiratorial looks.

"We were hoping Stu would show us around."

Elsa beamed with pride. "Yes, that's a great idea!" She turned to me. "Why don't you give the girls a tour. It will be a chance for you to get more familiar with the store's layout and merchandise."

Lucky me. All I needed was a pink parasol in one hand to make my morning complete. "Sure."

I led the girls on a quick lap of the store. "Over here are dresses and stuff. And over here are more dresses, and belts, and stuff. And over here are blouses, and shoes, and more dresses, and stuff." That seemed to pretty much wrap up the tour for me.

"What about over there?" Kirsten asked, pointing to the far corner I had conveniently avoided. She smiled innocently.

That girl was worse than Ben. I made a mental note never to let my guard down again in her presence.

"That's where the sundries are kept." I wasn't sure what the word *sundries* meant, but I hoped it covered what lurked in that corner.

"Sundries? What sort of sundries?" Kirsten's smile came straight from the devil.

"You know, like, swimsuits, and stuff."

"Oh," Becca added innocently. "What sort of stuff?"

If their plan was to embarrass me, it was working perfectly. Time to put an end to the foolishness. "You know, women's . . . brassieres, and stuff."

Kirsten and Becca doubled over. "Brassieres?"

"You know what I mean . . . women's undies, and stuff." I was sweating enough for the alligator on my shirt to submerge beneath the tropical stream flowing from my armpits.

Becca straightened up. "Yes, I think we know."

The alligator slipped downstream. Of course, they knew. "Funny. You guys are the best."

Becca bumped my shoulder. "Thanks for the tour. Your grandma has a really nice store."

"Yeah," Kirsten said. "Now we know where to come when we're in need of sundries."

From the way they giggled their way out the front door, I concluded the tour had been a great success, if only I were working in a comedy club. Unfortunately, I was working in a women's clothing store and the only thing funny here was me, and that was entirely by accident.

Elsa spent the next few days showing me how to work the cash register, complete a sale, empty the dressing rooms, refold clothes, tidy the display tables, and other things I never wanted to know. Thursday, as I was about to leave, she had me take her through the whole checkout process just like she was a real paying customer.

"Perfect, you've got it," she said as I gave her change from the cash register. "You're all set for tomorrow."

"What about tomorrow?"

Elsa stopped short. "Didn't I already tell you? I need to take my mom to the doctor tomorrow. You're going to be running the store on your own for a few hours."

Say what? "What do you mean, on my own?"

"Don't worry, Fridays are quiet. And you know everything you need to know. It's going to be fine."

"But I've never been alone in the store before."

"True," she said. "That's why tomorrow is going to be such a great day! And if you run into any trouble I'll have my cell phone on me, so just call."

She squinted at the fear plastered on my face.

"Stu, I can't skip her appointment. She's beginning to think I'm avoiding her on purpose." She held a hand close to her mouth to cover her words. "Which I am, but don't tell her."

With that, she shooed me out the door.

"Get a good night's rest. You'll want to be at your best for tomorrow!"

My best? My best what?

# 10

Friday morning came in all its dark and stormy fury, which was strange since there wasn't a cloud in the sky. I arrived at the store just in time for Elsa to hand me the keys and wave goodbye on her way out.

"Don't worry, it's going to be fine," she called over her shoulder.

Her words rang true until my first customer of the day entered. Diane was hard to miss wearing the sky-blue pantsuit from her last visit.

"Stu!" she said, taking my hand. "It's so good to see you again. How is your grandmother doing?"

"She's doing well, ma'am. She's at a care facility in Port Angeles for a couple weeks."

"Yes, so I've heard. I'm planning to stop by for a

visit tomorrow." She dabbed at one eye just like the last time. "She has the soul of an angel, your grandma. And the heart of a lion. I don't know what this town would do without her."

"Yeah, I can't wait for her to get back to her old self. And take over the store again." That last part might've been a bit selfish. But in my defense, I was the one wearing a pink polo shirt trying to make small talk with a woman five times my age.

Diane turned in a circle scanning the racks and tables. "Where's Elsa?"

"She's taking her mother to the doctor," I explained.

"That girl's mother is something else," she said, leafing through the dresses on one of the racks. "All she seems to care about is that Elsa find a man and settle down." She gave me a wink. "There's nothing wrong with men, mind you, but a woman doesn't need one to be all right. That girl knows how to take care of herself." She pulled out a dress with a feather pattern. "I've always loved paisley."

She carried the dress to the back of the store and

into the first dressing room. I idly straightened the hangers on the rack to keep myself occupied and to avoid thinking about what was going on in that room.

"Stu!" Diane called. "Sorry to bother but the zipper's stuck."

I scanned the store for the poor sap named Stu. My eyes landed on my own name tag. Oh, chipotle.

"Stu, dear!" Diane called again from her dressing room of death.

I found her standing with the door open and her back turned to me. The zipper on the paisley dress hung limply midway up her back. As best I could tell, the zipper had either tired from the climb or been frightened by the bulging mass of freckles looming up ahead. I could hardly blame the zipper for hunkering down. Diane reached behind with one hand and groped at the zipper, demonstrating how it wouldn't budge.

"Sorry, I need a little help with the last bit."

If anyone at any time had explained working at my grandmother's store would involve zipping women's zippers, I would have politely gone screaming for the hills. But that little secret was left for me to discover on my own. The zombie warlord turned away with a shudder as I gripped the metal tab and pulled upward.

The zipper climbed a couple inches, then ground to a halt. I desperately tried rocking it back and forth, but it refused to budge. On closer inspection, I discovered the edge of the dress had gotten sucked into the metal tines until the zipper and dress had become hopelessly entangled.

"Uh, I think the zipper's really stuck."

Diane reached back and stroked the zipper with one finger.

"Yep, looks like it's stuck good," she said. "You'll have to pull the material out of the zipper's teeth to free it."

And that's when I discovered a newfound hate for zipper designers. Pulling the material out required both hands. Against my will, my fingers rubbed against her back as I worked to free the zipper.

"I'm sorry. I didn't mean to make it worse." I also didn't mean to be giving her a back rub while wrestling half the dress out of the zipper's beastly jaws.

"Not to worry," she replied. "My late husband never could zip me up without it turning into an all-out brawl with the zipper." She dabbed at an eye. "I miss those days."

The material finally pulled free. This time I ignored my fear of her skin and carefully pulled the material out of the way so the zipper could zip freely all the way to the top. At last, I stepped back and studied my work. Before me stood one large, elderly woman now fully clothed in a lovely pink paisley dress.

"I'm sure he would have liked you in that dress," I said without thinking.

She turned and studied herself in the mirror. "He always liked me with a little meat on my bones. And he did always love my summer dresses." She turned to face me. "I'll take it."

And so, I made my first sale. And discovered that clothing isn't always about looking good. Sometimes it's about looking back and remembering how good you once looked. And who was around to notice it.

⁓

That evening, my parents took my brother and me to

visit my grandmother in the nursing home. She was as spirited as ever.

"I'm not staying here another night," she greeted us as we entered her room.

I couldn't really blame her. The nursing home smelled like the inside of my gym locker.

"Try and be patient," my father cooed. "It's just for a couple weeks while they help you rehab your repaired hip. And then you'll go home."

My grandmother scowled. "I'll be dead in this place before then."

My mother sat on the edge of the bed and took one of my grandmother's hands. "We promise we won't let anything happen to you here. Just hang in there and you'll be home soon."

"Easy for you to say, you're sleeping in your own bed in the land of the living. I'm here in the halls of borrowed time. Can you believe they gave me vegetarian lasagna for lunch? What sort of place is this?"

Clearly, she belonged in our family. My father held up a paper bag.

"Guessing you won't mind what I got you here."

She tore the bag open. Out came a beautifully cooked chicken leg along with a plastic container filled with mashed potatoes.

"You are your father's son," she said, biting into the chicken leg. "And the best child I never actually birthed."

My father beamed. "I think she's going to pull through."

She looked over at me. "So, how's the store holding up?"

Better than I was. "I made my first sale today, to Diane."

"Well, I'll be," she said with real admiration. "That woman is a wonder. Did you know her husband passed away unexpectedly about a year ago? She refused to leave the house for a month. Elsa and I took turns bringing the latest inventory to her so we could check on her and make sure she didn't stay holed up there forever." She took my hand. "That's what customer service is all about. Meet the customer's need before they know they have one."

No wonder Diane thought so highly of her.

"She said you had the soul of an angel."

My grandmother leaned back in the bed. "I can tell you right now I'm no angel." She tore off another bite of chicken, skin and all. "But I do care about the customers I serve. And they seem to appreciate that."

That was for darn sure.

# 11

Saturday morning a chill hung in the store as if the AC had been left on all night. Elsa sat behind the cash register, her usual cheery attitude replaced by a long face not unlike the look she had been wearing yesterday when she returned from the doctor.

"Good morning," she mumbled.

Her gray blouse shouted that the morning was anything but good. She had forgotten to wear something pink. My own polo shirt glowed with all the pinkness of a summer sunrise. Something had to be up. What she needed was a perceptive leading question to help her open up. But I had no idea what sort of perceptive leading question to ask. Instead, I wandered the aisles testing out my new theory that I could make time move faster by blinking.

Elsa trailed me as I made my way around the store. If I didn't know better, I'd think she was waiting for me to ask her a perceptive leading question. My brain let out an audible sigh.

"How's your mom?" I tried.

And that's when I learned that asking Elsa a perceptive leading question was less important than asking her any question at all.

"She's fine. She spent yesterday telling me about the new blood pressure medication her doctor put her on. And about the arthritis medication she's refusing to take. And about how her feet keep swelling up at night. And how the other evening when she went out for dinner with friends the shrimp tasted overcooked and her asparagus was stringy."

She picked up a blouse from the display on her right and idly refolded it.

"And don't even get me started on the earful she gave me about settling down."

She unfolded and refolded the blouse again. A follow-up question seemed in order, but I was as good with follow-up questions as I was with perceptive leading questions. I blinked in the vain attempt to hurry morning into afternoon.

"My mom is so old-fashioned," she continued. "She thinks all that matters is finding a man, staying home, and pumping out a few kids." She unfolded the blouse and refolded it for the third time. "My mother never worked a day outside the home in her life. She has no idea what it means to have a career or even to get an education."

My blinking theory failed miserably. Time was moving so slowly I'd be old and gray before the clock hit 2:00 p.m.

"I haven't even told her I'm going to night school to get a degree in business."

She looked up at me with a sincerity that actually made my eyes stop blinking.

"It was your grandmother's idea. I never even thought about going to college after high school. But she encouraged me it wasn't too late and that I could do it. She's even paying my tuition. She's like that. She does things for people all the time and never lets on about it." She wiped away the mascara streaking down one cheek.

What was with women sniffling every time they

talked about my grandmother? Though she did seem pretty saintly the more I learned about her. To be honest, I had never really thought about my grandmother much before. My only impression was that she seemed busy with the store all the time and that every now and then she'd pull out a magic trick that seemed like real magic. Oh, and the holiday money. Not just a card with two dollars inside and a note that read *Save this for college*, like Ben's grandma did. My grandma put serious money in her cards.

"Well, time to get back to things. Thanks for listening to me blubber."

The temperature in the store warmed up after that, and the rest of the morning went by quicker than I expected. Maybe the blinking worked after all.

On my way out, I broached the question that I had been avoiding.

"Would it be possible to leave a little early tomorrow?"

Elsa took a sip from her coffee mug. "After covering for me yesterday, I think the least I can do is give you tomorrow off. Whatcha got going on?"

Hmm . . . how to answer her question without giving away what was actually happening? "Not much, a family picnic."

"Oh, that sounds like fun. Where is your family going?"

From recent experience, I had learned honesty is the best policy. Little lies had a funny way of escalating into bigger lies that ended with me wearing a potato costume in front of the whole school. "Lake Crescent." Okay, maybe I didn't correct her assumption about the picnic being with my family. But technically I didn't lie, either.

"Wait, isn't your mom going to the hospital auxiliary board meeting tomorrow afternoon?"

Oh, ship. "Well, I'm actually going with a friend and her family."

The word *her* slipped out before I could stop it. Elsa froze. I could see her mind whirring, piecing together the puzzle. Recognition lit up her face.

"Is *she* one of the girls who came into the store Monday?"

I wished desperately for detachable ears. At the moment, mine were heating up like a pottery oven. "Maybe."

"They both seemed like nice young ladies."

Obviously, she didn't know Kirsten. "Yeah, I guess so."

The front door opened, and a little lady with a bright red arm bag entered. Elsa headed her direction.

"Have fun!" she called over her shoulder. "You'll have to tell me all about it Monday."

I could hardly wait.

**12**

At dinner that evening, my father called me over to the BBQ, where he was happily flipping burgers.

"Your mother tells me you're going on a picnic tomorrow."

Now why would my mother have told my father something like that? "Yeah."

"Things are getting a little more serious with this girl."

Really, they weren't. Were they? "We're friends."

He finished flipping a row of burgers, then gave me a raised eyebrow.

"Your mother says her whole family will be going on the picnic. Is that right?"

Something about his questions woke a few moths and a butterfly that had been lying dormant in my stomach. "I guess so."

He nodded. "Dads can be kinda funny about their daughters. If he asks you any questions, just stay calm and be yourself. You'll do fine."

Questions? What sort of questions? Nobody said there would be an interview portion of the picnic. Up to now, I had stayed surprisingly calm about the idea of spending the day with Becca and her family. But something about my father's words felt like a warning. "Okay."

That night after I crawled into bed, I imagined the cabin in the woods with Becca hiding inside sur-rounded by zombies. The nightly rescue usually soothed me to sleep. But not this night. This time the zombies were replaced by a creature far more menacing than any zombie I had ever encountered, a creature so fierce I abandoned the rescue and ran screaming until a tree root sent me sprawling to the ground. The creature stood over me, blood dripping from its massive jaws. "I have a few questions," it growled. "And I expect answers."

So much for a good night's sleep.

I woke Sunday morning in an upbeat, chipper mood. Not really. In reality, I woke with a stomach full of butterflies that threatened to lift me out of bed and whisk me out my bedroom window. Being whisked away by a mass of butterflies seemed like a pretty good idea. Anything to avoid being interrogated by Becca's werewolf father for real. Honestly, I did have a way of exaggerating things. The afternoon couldn't possibly be as bad as last night. Right?

On the slim chance that the day could be as bad as last night, I pulled out a pen and paper and brainstormed excuses I could use to get out of going.

"Stu," my mother called. "It's eleven. Aren't you supposed to be at Becca's house?"

What? Where had the last two hours gone? I

reviewed the list of excuses I had compiled. *Because I'm a coward* had been crossed off, along with *Your father is a werewolf, and not the vegetarian kind, either.* That left a blank page full of nothing. I hadn't thought of a single excuse that Becca would accept.

It looked like there was only once choice left: join a witness protection program. Ben and I once watched a movie where the main character was given a new identity and relocated to a faraway town after testifying against the mob. If only I knew a crime family I could testify against. Unfortunately, Sequim's a bit short on gangsters. I pulled on my sneakers and headed over to Becca's house.

I found her waiting on the porch.

"I'm glad you made it," she said. "I was starting to get a little worried."

That's where our worrying differed. Her worry ended with my arrival. Mine wouldn't end until either I arrived home safely or was ingested by her werewolf father as a midday snack. "Wouldn't have missed it."

She led me through the house and out back where the rest of the family had already loaded into their

SUV. Her little sister, Carly, had already claimed the middle seat in back, which left Becca to sit on one side of her and me on the other.

"I'm glad you could join us," Becca's mother said.

"Thank you for inviting me," I replied with all the politeness I could muster.

"Hmpth," Becca's father said, shifting into gear.

We headed out of town on Highway 101 with the windows down and a song from the '80s blaring on the radio. The singer kept repeating "I can't drive fifty-five." Apparently, Becca's father could. The last time I was in a vehicle going this slow was the bumper cars at the Irrigation Festival's carnival. The memory brought a shiver.

"Does your family go to Lake Crescent often?" Becca's mother yelled over the music.

"No," I yelled back. "I've only been there a couple of times."

"Oh," she said. "We think the lake is the most beautiful spot on the Peninsula."

"Becca likes you," Carly chimed in.

Becca jabbed Carly in the side with her elbow. "Shut up."

Becca's mom turned in her seat.

"Remember what we talked about, Carly. You are to conduct yourself like a mature young lady."

Carly beamed up at me with innocent eyes.

"Sorry." She lowered her voice just enough that the music prevented anyone else from hearing her but me. "I like when Jackson comes over. He brings me pictures he's drawn of ninja kittens and stuff."

Her words struck me like a zombie slap in the face. Jackson had been over to their house? The zombie warlord pounded to get out, probably so he could slap me, too. Here I'd spent the night worrying about her werewolf father when I should have been worrying about a far more sinister creature from the deep, one with real biceps and a lone chin hair.

The rest of the ride was pretty much the worst. How was a guy supposed to enjoy a summer outing with his girlfriend when he wasn't even sure she *was* his girlfriend? My mind whirled with the possibilities. Had she and Jackson been secretly dating? Or were they openly dating and no one had thought to tell me? Or could there be a bigger dating conspiracy going on involving dozens of my classmates bound by secret handshakes and techno cool spy gadgets? Okay, that idea sounded a bit wacko. But if something was going on, where did it leave me? Was I just the guy Becca felt too sorry for to tell the crushing truth? No, she would never lie to me. Or would she? Truth be told, I might have set a bad precedent in the spring. But she wasn't still holding that against me, was she?

The car came to a stop in the parking lot next to the Lake Crescent Lodge.

"We're here," Becca's mother announced.

We climbed out of the SUV and took a collective moment to ooh and aah at the lake. Before us Lake Crescent stretched for twelve miles surrounded by evergreen wooded hills with the Olympic Mountains rising in the background. The setting reminded me of photos I'd seen of the Scottish lochs, except no castles or Loch Ness monsters here.

We walked out on the dock in front of the lodge.

The water was so clear you could see submerged logs lying at the bottom. You could also see how the bottom dropped from shallow to scary deep in the matter of a few steps. Scientists had calculated the deepest point at over six hundred feet, but rumor held that the real depth was more like a thousand. I could believe it. From the end of the dock, the lake looked bottomless.

"The water is clear because it lacks enough nitrogen for algae to grow," Becca's father said.

Becca and I reached down and touched the water with our fingertips. Even in the summer, it felt ice-cold.

"Anyone want to go swimming?" Becca's mother asked.

"No," Becca said, shaking her hand dry. "You'd have to be a polar bear to swim in this lake."

"I left my polar bear suit at home," I added.

We sauntered back and unloaded supplies from the SUV for our picnic. Becca's family knew how to do a picnic right. They had blankets, camping chairs, beach toys, baskets of food, and a cooler with wheels that I pulled behind me until we found a perfect spot on the lawn not far from the lodge.

"Can I wade in the water?" Carly asked.

"Just for a few minutes," Becca's mother replied. "We're going to eat soon."

I busied myself watching Becca and her parents set up camp. I would have gladly helped, but I had no idea how. They worked in unison, as if going on a picnic were some sort of elaborate folk dance.

"Wow," I murmured.

"Do you like it?" Becca asked, surveying their work. "I made sure we brought things you would eat." She pointed to the sandwiches. "Half are peanut butter. And we also brought deviled eggs, and potato chips, and your favorite"—she pointed to a bowl of fiery death—"Joe's Smokin' Peas."

"Love those smokin' peas," I agreed, feigning I was about to vomit.

"Carly!" Becca's mother called. "Time to eat."

We gathered in a circle on the blanket like the lords and ladies the picnic demanded. I even placed a napkin in my lap on the off chance I remembered to use it. This was what picnicking was meant to be. Gourmet food, a comfy blanket, and a leisurely afternoon spent with friends and family. I raised a deviled egg in toast, then jammed it into my mouth.

"So, what are your plans for the future?" Becca's father asked.

The deviled egg lodged in midswallow. The last thing I needed was another explosive food spewing moment like the day I first met Becca. My father's warning returned to mind. Stay calm and be myself, that's what he'd advised. Which made sense if only I knew who I was and how to stay calm in the presence of a werewolf masquerading as Becca's dad.

"Mbtthf," I sputtered. The strangled sound was both all I could force past the egg and all I knew of my future plans.

"Bill," Becca's mother said. "Is this really the time?"

Becca's father took a swig of his Lane's All-Natural Cream Soda. "I was just asking the boy a question."

True, what harm could there be in asking a thirteen-year-old boy his plans for the future? Didn't all boys my age already have their lives planned out? Come to think of it, just this morning I had almost made the life decision to enter the witness protection program. Maybe it wasn't too late.

"Becca tells me you like to play soccer," Becca's mother interjected, trying to steer the conversation in a safer direction.

"Jackson is a really good goalkeeper," Carly threw out. "I can almost never score on him, and I'm a good scorer."

Becca stiffened. "Carly and Jess are best friends," she explained quickly.

Great. Jackson's little sister was Carly's best friend. What a perfect excuse for him to come over and hang out. The four of them were probably going to the park every day and playing soccer while I was busy in my grandmother's store selling sundries to old ladies.

I was beginning to wonder if I'd done something to anger the universe. It seemed like every time I started to feel good about my life, some higher power threw down a meat float or a pink paisley pantsuit to squash me in my tracks.

Please God, give a guy a break.

14

"Want to go for a hike?" Becca asked after we'd finished eating.

"Sure." A quick jaunt up Mount Everest seemed perfect right about now.

"Don't go too far," her mother said. "We need to head home in about an hour."

"Don't worry," Becca replied. "We're just going to walk the loop trail."

Her father gave me a slack-jawed disapproving look. One fang glistened in the sunlight.

Thank goodness he wasn't the one taking me into the woods.

"C'mon," Becca said. "Let's go."

We wandered across a big grassy area to where a trail entered the woods. The farther we got away from her werewolf father and her Jackson-admiring little sister the more I relaxed.

"Dad said I had to go with you."

Carly ran to catch up. Becca grunted.

"Do you really have to come with us?"

Carly picked up a stick and dragged it across the ferns on the side of the trail.

"He said, 'Stay close and keep an eye on those two.' Mom said, 'Not too close,' whatever that means."

She skipped ahead humming merrily, her stick thudding across the wincing ferns in her path.

"Sorry," Becca whispered. "My parents can be such a pain."

We reached an open area where the trail passed by a small beach. Carly waded in up to her ankles, then spun with her stick sending water splashing around her.

"Look! I'm a little hurricane!" she shouted.

Becca and I sat on a log at one end of the beach.

"She's right about that," Becca said. "She is a little hurricane."

"Maybe there's a creature in the lake like the Loch

Ness monster," I suggested. "One that eats the occa-sional little hurricane for lunch. If we can just lure her a little farther from shore."

"It's worth a shot," Becca replied. "Then I could have my room back."

"Your parents might be sad."

"Yeah, I suppose. But I could get them a puppy. A puppy would be cuter and more fun to play with and wouldn't talk all the time."

"True. I'd trade my little brother for a puppy any day."

Becca picked up a rock and tossed it into the water.

"Hey, my thirteenth birthday is in August. I was thinking of having a party. Do you think I should have it at my house?"

"I guess so, or maybe at a park."

A smile lit up her face.

"That's a great idea. We'll have it at Sequim Bay State Park! We can make s'mores."

"Yeah, those vegetarian s'mores were a hit at my house."

"That's it! We'll have a picnic, and then a bonfire with s'mores! It's perfect!"

It did sound pretty fun. Right up until I got to Ben's house that night.

"Dude, you won't believe the day I've had!" Ben announced the moment we sat down near his Xbox.

"What are you talking about?"

"We kissed!"

"What do you mean you kissed? I thought she was mad at you."

"Yeah, I know. She was."

Ben's grin looked bigger than his head if that was even possible.

"She called me and wanted to get together and talk so we met at the park near her house. I was pretty nervous about seeing her after what went down at ice cream the other day. But she was really cool about it. She told me her mom's been giving her a bad time about her grades lately."

He looked at me with actual sincerity.

"Her mom sounds crazy. She thinks Kirsten should get straight As or she won't get into a good college."

"That does seem crazy."

"Yeah, she's super intense about everything Kirsten does. She's making her take all honors classes next year even though those grades don't even count toward her high school GPA."

I tried to imagine my parents being that worried about my grades. My life would be a nightmare.

"Whoa. How does Kirsten deal with it?"

"It's pretty hard sometimes. She started crying while we were talking."

That brought back the memory of Becca on the steps in front of her house. Girls were complicated.

"So, what did you do?"

Ben downed the last chips in the bag he was holding, then crushed the bag with one hand.

"At first, I didn't know what to do. It was kinda weird, her all teary and stuff. And then I told her about how my parents are always on me about school. I wish sometimes they'd just leave me alone. And she said she wished her mom would just leave her alone. And then—and then we kissed."

"What?"

"Yeah, I know. It was like we were having this real moment talking about our parents. And then . . . it just . . . sort of happened."

The zombie warlord tapped out a reminder how Becca and I had had a similar talk only days before. Could things turn all smoochy that easily?

"Dude, I'm telling you. It was amazing!"

I didn't remember asking a follow-up question.

"It was like—like that level in *Death Intruders* where we were forced to marry zombie brides and then they kissed us. Remember that?"

Um, yeah. My character was still collecting bits of his skull blown off in the explosion.

"Seriously, I thought my head was going to explode. It was so awesome!"

Since when did having your head explode become awesome?

"You're next, dude."

Seriously, the last thing I needed after facing Becca's werewolf father and her sister's Jackson revelations was to be stressed out about some looming kiss.

"Yeah, right."

"No, seriously. It's awesome. You just need a special moment to set the mood."

"We did plan her birthday party for August."

"Perfect!" A wicked gleam lit up his eyes. "If she waits that long."

Just what I needed to hear.

**16**

When I got to work on Monday, I found Elsa waiting with eager eyes.

"How did your date go?" she asked.

"I had a picnic with her family," I answered, skillfully avoiding giving away anything of interest.

"C'mon," she persisted. "You gotta give me more details than that."

So much for skillful avoidance.

"Well, we went to Lake Crescent and had a picnic by the lodge. Her father asked me what my plans were for the future."

Her eager eyes widened into alarm.

"He asked you about your plans for the future?" She gave an eye roll that would've made my mother proud. "That seems a bit premature. You're thirteen and the two of you just started dating."

That's exactly what I thought, except for the dating part.

"And her little sister told me that another boy has been coming over."

Her alarmed look widened to a whole other level of alarmed.

"No! That can't be. She's too sweet to be two-timing on you."

What exactly did Elsa know about Becca? They had only met briefly once. Maybe she had psychic powers. Ben and I used to watch a show about a girl with psychic powers. She could read other people's thoughts and could even move things with her mind. Ben tried for months to move a pencil with his mind until his parents finally figured out he wasn't turning in any of his math assignments. Psychic powers are still banned at his house.

"I don't know. Jackson is bigger than I am and has better grades. And he never does stupid things around her."

She put her hands on her hips.

"And that's why he's wrong for her. She deserves a guy whose palms get sweaty and his words get all mixed up around her. That's the guy who's really smitten."

Based on her definition, I was definitely smitten.

The next hour I spent working in the back room. One thing I had learned about a clothing store is that stuff is always coming and going. That means a lot of boxes with a lot of clothes to be opened, sorted, and displayed. At the moment, I had about a dozen boxes and three hours of time. Opening four boxes an hour would be a challenge, but one that I was more than willing to accept.

"Stu! You're needed by a customer."

The odds of me being needed by a customer seemed slim at best. It was more likely Elsa trying to boost my confidence as a sales consultant. The box cutter went back up on the shelf.

Near the front door, I found an elderly lady with gray hair and skin so wrinkled she looked like she had just taken the world's longest bath.

"Stu, I'd like you to meet Ms. Helperdin. She's a friend of Diane's."

Ms. Helperdin took my hand.

"Diane told me you are the one who can help me find a dress for my Charles's ninetieth birthday party."

Why on earth would Diane have said something like that? I couldn't even get her zipper zipped. The memory sent a shiver up my spine.

Elsa smiled. "I was just telling Ms. Helperdin what an asset you are to the store. I'll leave you two to find something amazing."

I stood next to Ms. Helperdin and tried not to look as awkward as I felt, though I was pretty sure I looked exactly that awkward. I didn't know anything about women's tastes in clothing. And the last thing I wanted to do on a sunny Sequim morning was traipse around the store with a wrinkly little old lady. All I needed was for Ben to pop up from inside a rack of blouses to make my embarrassment complete.

"Um, what sort of dress are you looking for?" I asked. Not that her answer would in any way help, since the racks of dresses all looked the same to me.

Ms. Helperdin shuffled farther into the store.

"My Charles and I met when we were thirteen."

That got my attention. They had known each other for seventy-seven years? I couldn't fathom knowing anyone that long. I'd known Ben for ten years, and that already seemed long enough.

"Wow, that's a really long time."

She skimmed her hand over a rack of dresses.

"Yes, we met during World War II. His mother moved to Seattle to work for Boeing making bombers. He showed up in class one day, and I thought he was so handsome."

She ran a finger down the sleeve of a black velvet evening gown.

"We went to our first dance together. I wore a velvet dress, and he wore a suit two sizes too large. We were inseparable that night. And have been ever since."

I pulled the dress from the rack. It was much too large for someone so small and frail, but her fingers refused to let go of the fabric.

"Would you like me to see if I can find one in your size?" I suggested.

Elsa, who had been watching from the cash register, pulled the same dress in a smaller size from the far side of the circular rack.

"Try this," she offered, handing me the dress.

I escorted Ms. Helperdin to the dressing room.

"I'm going to need a little help," Ms. Helperdin said before stepping inside. "I think Elsa will be best now."

I breathed a sigh of relief as Elsa stepped into the dressing room with Ms. Helperdin and closed the door.

A few minutes later, the door opened, and Ms. Helperdin emerged. My mouth gaped. She looked thirty years younger. I'm not sure whether it was the dress or the too-pleased smile lighting up her face when she caught me staring at her.

"Do you think he'll like it?" she asked.

I suddenly wondered when I turned ninety if anyone would care if I liked what they were wearing. "Yes, I think so."

Ms. Helperdin turned to Elsa.

"Would you mind helping me take this thing off? And do you have a box I could take it home in? I'd like it to be a surprise."

After she changed, I walked her to her car carrying the box with the new dress inside.

"He wrote me a poem," she said, easing herself into the driver's seat. "After the dance."

"Oh, that's nice."

She giggled. "It wasn't a good poem, mind you. He compared me to his bicycle. And a seagull. And a yellow daffodil. I still have it in a drawer."

With a final wave she drove off, fond memories and new black dress tucked safely next to her.

Elsa stood waiting at the door when I returned.

"Well, that was about the cutest thing ever!" she exclaimed, ushering me inside. "You and Ms. Helperdin shopping for a birthday party dress together. If only I'd gotten it on video."

That was about the last thing I wanted. "I didn't really do anything. She picked out the dress herself."

"I know!" Elsa almost shouted. "But you listened to her and cared. And that's what led her to the right dress. You're a genius!"

Say what?

# 17

That night, we made another visit to see my grandmother at the nursing home. She greeted us just as chipper as the last time.

"I gotta get out of this place," she stated the moment we entered.

"Soon enough," my father soothed.

She stuck out her chin and slumped back in bed. It was the first time since the accident I had seen her move without wincing.

"I don't know how anyone is supposed to sleep in this place with all the moaning and groaning at night. I think it must be haunted."

My father held out a roast beef sandwich on rye that my grandmother tore into like a half-starved inmate.

The smell of mustard wafted about the room.

"I'm serious," she said between mouthfuls. "And whoever is wandering the halls didn't die peacefully, either."

"That's Mr. Tallsfelder," a nurse said, entering with a cup of water and a handful of pills. "He moans in his sleep. Don't worry, he's really quite fine and still very much alive."

The nurse watched to make sure my grandmother swallowed the pills, then breezed back out of the room.

"I don't trust that woman," my grandmother said after the nurse had left. "She's always so pleasant."

My mother patted my grandmother's hand.

"I believe they are trained to be pleasant. Would you rather she barked at you?"

"Frankly, I'd feel more at ease with a drill sergeant for a nurse than a sweet-talking, pill-pushing young woman telling me lies to keep me quiet. Very much alive, is he? Very much alive my—"

"Well," my father interrupted. "Your doctor tells me you're healing so quick that she expects you'll be going home early. Just hang in there for a couple more days."

My grandmother gnawed on the hard-crust remains of her sandwich.

"Yes, they keep saying that. But I think it's just a trick to keep me compliant. I bet they told Mr. Tallsfelder the same thing a few years ago. Look at him now, haunting and moaning every night. They probably keep his ghost locked up so they can still collect fees from his insurance."

My father let out a heavy sigh.

"Well, your hip may be broken, but your imagination is as fit as ever."

"Stu made another sale today," my mother interjected.

That brought a light to my grandmother's eyes.

"Is that right?" she said. "I'm not surprised. You come from a long line of salespeople."

What was she talking about? I came from a long line of butchers. Not a lot of sales involved in cutting up slabs of meat into smaller slabs of meat. But then again, I guess my father did run a store and helped customers get what they needed. I'd never really thought about my father being a salesperson before.

"You're right about that," my father agreed. "The Truly name has long been associated with sales and service in this town."

"And meat," I added.

"Yes, and meat," my father repeated with a grin. "Amen to that."

My grandmother motioned me closer. She sat up straighter and took my hand.

"Tell me the truth," she said. "The fashion show is happening in five weeks. Has Elsa worked on any of the arrangements yet?"

"Um . . . I'm not really sure. She hasn't really talked about it much."

My grandmother let out a slow sigh. "She's a very good store manager. But she struggles with follow-through when it comes to event planning. Truth is, I could make the arrangements from here, but if she's going to take over the store when I retire, she's got to learn to stand on her own two feet."

"So, she really is going to take over the store?" I asked.

My grandmother held her water glass up in toast.

"I sure hope so. One thing my hip has shown me is that I'm not getting any younger. I'm getting the itch to do a little traveling and not be hitched to that store seven days a week."

She gripped my hand tight.

"That's why I need you to make sure she follows through. Can you do that?"

I wasn't really sure what my grandmother was asking of me. But how could I say no to her? "Okay."

⌢

That night at bedtime my mother stopped by to tuck me in. She still gave me a hug and kiss every night even though I had been trying for months to put an end to the practice. However, since she happened to be sitting on the edge of the bed, it seemed like as good a time as any to ask the embarrassing question that had been plaguing me ever since the picnic.

"If you were getting a birthday present for a girl, what would you get?"

That stopped my mother cold. She straightened up and pursed her lips as if trying to decide whether to answer the question or go back to pretending her little boy was still five years old.

"Well, that's not a question with an easy answer. Is this about Becca?"

Why does a simple question always have to be made into something more complicated? "Maybe."

"I see. How soon is her birthday?"

"August."

"Well, at least you're getting started early."

She rested her chin on her hand.

"Hmm . . . you haven't been together for very long, so this is not the time to break the bank and get something extravagant."

That was a relief. But since I didn't know the difference between extravagant and non-extravagant girl gifts it didn't really answer the question. "What sort of gift did Dad get you?"

She stifled a laugh. "Your father fancied himself a romantic. He used to write me poems."

Hey, that's what Mrs. Helperdin said her husband did. "Do you remember any of them?"

A blush crept up my mother's face.

"Not any I'm going to repeat to you."

She tousled my hair, then stood and headed for the door.

"If I think of any ideas I'll let you know."

I lay in bed and thought about Becca's birthday. Both my father and Mr. Helperdin had written poems. Maybe that was the answer. After all, I had written loads of words on paper. And had made up rhymes mocking the size of Ben's head lots of times. How hard could writing a poem for Becca be?

The next morning, I found Elsa hunched over the counter next to the cash register with a pad of paper in front of her and a pen dangling from her fingers. She looked like she hadn't slept.

"Hey, Stu," she said.

I hated to ask the obvious for fear of being forced to listen to the answer, but I had learned Elsa wasn't the type to keep anything secret. I was going to hear about it whether I wanted to or not. "What are you working on?"

"I stopped by and visited your grandmother last evening. I think it was right after your family had been there."

She stared down at the blank sheet of paper in front of her.

"We talked a lot about the fashion show and how quickly the date is coming up. Your grandmother gave me a lot of input on what needs to be done to get ready."

The pen clunked onto the counter.

"I should have taken notes. Now I can't remember anything we went over."

She tried to take a deep breath, but the air caught in her throat. I had never really thought about how adults can be given assignments in real life just like kids are given in school. And apparently they can feel just as confused and overwhelmed. I reached over and picked up the pen and notepad.

"Maybe if you talk it out I can write down notes for you."

The idea popped out of my mouth before I had time to think through the consequences. The all-too-eager look on Elsa's face made it clear I couldn't go back now.

"That'd be great!" Elsa enthused. "I can't seem to think and write at the same time."

Every English paper I had ever been assigned jumped to mind. "Yeah, I feel you there."

Elsa spent the next hour bubbling about the fashion

show. Whatever she lacked in event-planning skills she more than made up for with enthusiasm. My hand got tired from scribbling notes.

"And at the end I'll have your grandmother come up onstage and say a few words. I'm hoping the show can coincide with her returning to work. The audience will go wild when they realize she's all healed and back to stay."

Elsa leaned on the counter, panting from the exertion of talking nonstop for so long. I stretched my aching fingers, then dropped the pad on the counter next to her.

"I'm not sure I got everything you said or whether you'll be able to read my writing. But hopefully it helps."

She scanned the pages of notes.

"It's perfect. Everything is here. I just need to organize it and make a plan of action."

"Right. While you're working on that, I'll get to work on the boxes in back that need to be opened."

I spent the next two hours blissfully slitting tape while Elsa remained hunched over the counter, editing my notes and humming gleefully to herself.

About the time my fingers went numb from holding the box cutter, a thunderous rumble rolled up the street. A moment later, the bell on the front door jangled. I peeked out from the backroom to discover my dad's best friend, Harley, standing in the entry holding a brown paper bag. He seemed out of place in a store filled with pinks and yellows and reds. In contrast, he stood tall, broad shouldered, dressed all in black, with black greasy hair, and a black handlebar mustache.

Elsa approached cautiously.

"May I help you?"

Harley caught sight of Elsa and froze. I could see his lips trying to move but no sound came out.

"Um—I—uh—"

For a moment, I thought he might be having a stroke. But there was something strangely familiar about the look on his face and the way his words came out all jumbled.

"Hey, Harley," I said, joining them.

The moment he saw me, his face relaxed. It was as if seeing me broke some sort of spell he was under.

"Oh, hey, Stu."

He held out the bag.

"I was just visiting your dad at the butcher shop, and he asked me to bring you this."

Inside the bag, I found a ham sandwich on wheat bread with mustard oozing out in all directions. My mouth salivated.

"Thanks! This is awesome. I'm starving!"

Harley continued to stand in place, his eyes locked on Elsa. The goofy look on his face returned. I suddenly realized Elsa had a similar goofy look on her face. What was going on here?

"Elsa, this is my dad's friend Harley."

A blush crept up her face that threatened to catch her whole head on fire. She shyly held out a hand.

"It's nice to meet you," she said, her eyes all dreamy.

"Y-yes," Harley stammered, taking her hand in his.

The truth hit me like a rotting zombie arm to the head. They liked each other. Yikes. Were adults as awkward as kids about this sort of thing?

"Would you like to see the store while you're here?" Elsa asked.

"That'd be fine, real fine," Harley replied.

He followed behind her like a six-foot-five handlebar-mustached puppy.

"Maybe you'll find something for that special woman in your life," she said, catching his eye.

Even *I* knew where that was going. Harley blushed. Seriously, I didn't know a guy so tall, dark, and mustached could suddenly look so little and awkward. Whatever hold Elsa had on him was for real.

"I'm afraid there is no little lady in my life," he replied in a voice so shy it could have passed for my own.

I turned away. I couldn't bear to watch someone I idolized melt into such a pathetic puddle.

Unfortunately, the store wasn't big enough for me to avoid overhearing them while eating my sandwich. I learned that Harley grew up in Sequim while Elsa had only moved here a few years ago. I also learned that neither of them had dated in a long time and both enjoyed the weather in Sequim and the friendly, small-town attitude of the people. All the pleasant talk was enough to ruin my perfectly good ham sandwich. And then things took a really crazy turn.

"So, like I was telling you," Elsa babbled away, "I'm in charge of the fashion show this year with Rosemarie still recovering from her hip surgery. I don't know if I can do it. Rosemarie makes stuff like this look so easy. But I don't know how I'm going to get everything done on my own."

That's when the real shocker happened.

"Well," Harley replied, "I'd be happy to help."

My sandwich landed with a *thud* on the floor. Had Harley just offered to help put on a women's fashion show? My head swam from the implications. On the one hand, having Harley around the store would be great. He had a way about him that always made me feel better about myself. On the other hand, whatever was going on between the two of them would likely continue, and I'd be an innocent bystander forced to watch.

I picked up what remained of my sandwich and tossed it in the garbage. So much for my appetite.

# 19

That night I buckled down to get some real work done, real poetry work that is. The task seemed easy enough. Write a poem that delicately acknowledged my feelings for Becca while maintaining a manly sense of cool. Oh, and bonus points if it included the words *happy birthday* tucked neatly inside one of the lines.

I sat on my bed with my notebook and wrote whatever came to mind. Actually, nothing came to mind. Every time an idea started to work its way into my brain, I quickly squashed it, positive that it was the worst idea ever. This method led to a lot of squashing and very little writing. The longer I racked my brain for an idea, the more I became convinced that the only ideas my brain could muster were perfect for making fun of Ben's head but absolutely terrible for making Becca's birthday special.

In desperation, I resorted to the old standby *roses are red and violets are blue.* Maybe not the most original idea, but at least it gave me the first two lines. The remaining two lines were mine to fill in as I pleased, so long as the last word rhymed with *blue.* All I needed were approximately seven words to convey my heartfelt feeling that she was pretty much the coolest girl on the planet. Like a major-league pitcher, I wound up and threw out my first pitch.

*Roses are red*
*and violets are blue.*
*I think you're really cool,*
*coo coo ca choo.*

I read back what I had just written. My hand reflexively slapped my forehead. Coo coo ca choo? Where did that come from? A kindergartner could write better than that. I closed my eyes and tried again, this time slowing my mind and trusting my instincts. When I'd finished, I opened my eyes and read the words that had oozed straight out of my subconscious.

*Roses are red*

*and violets are blue.*

*If I had a dollar*

*I'd give it to you.*

What the—? What sort of pointless drivel was that? My other hand slapped my head. There was something seriously wrong with my subconscious. How was a guy to write the perfect poem if his subconscious was out to get him?

I forced myself to relax. All I needed were two perfect lines. In fact, I'd settle for two reasonably decent lines. Even two not-completely-dorky lines would be okay. It couldn't be that hard. I just needed to be confident in my poetic skills. No frills, no games, just two heartfelt lines that captured the entirety of my feelings. My hand pressed down, and words flowed freely as if some inner magic had been released.

*Roses are red*

*and violets are blue.*

*You have nice hair*

*and good teeth, too.*

I ducked to avoid both slapping hands. After three pathetic attempts, I was forced to admit I had the poetic sensibilities of a plastic garden gnome, which was unfair to plastic garden gnomes. How could I give Becca a poem if the best I could do was remind her she had good teeth?

"Stu!" my father called from downstairs. "Harley is having a get-together at his place tomorrow night for the Fourth of July. Tommy and I are going to get some fireworks. Want to come with us?"

Hmm . . . let's see. Stay here and continue to slap myself silly trying to write a poem that can't possibly be written. Or go with my father and brother to buy fireworks.

The notebook landed on the floor next to the pen. Maybe tomorrow I'd have better luck. For the moment, buying sparkly exploding things seemed like just the distraction I needed.

"Hang on! Don't go without me!"

**20**

A Fourth of July get-together at Harley's was a bit like a church picnic crossed with a firefight. People had brought more food than could possibly be eaten. And enough fireworks to burn the town down twice. Revelers wandered the yard eating BBQ and commenting on what a lovely summer it had been so far.

I found the meat float crew huddled together near the barn reminiscing about the good old day, and I do mean *day*, when they were the hit of the festival parade.

"Remember when I wound up with the bat and knocked the living daylights out of that papier-mâché bunny?" my father's friend Joe boasted. "Red licorice exploded all over the crowd. It was awesome, man!"

Having been on the parade float with him when it

happened, *awesome* is not the word I would have used. Disgusting maybe, deeply disturbing perhaps, but not awesome. I'm pretty sure there were kids in the crowd still in therapy after being sprayed with what looked like licorice blood from an exploding bunny rabbit.

"Yeah," my dad quipped. "The crowd pretty much went nuts for us. The store has been hopping ever since."

True, once I took the bat away from Joe, the crowd pretty much did love us. There are probably photos of me in my rack of ribs costume and Tommy in his chicken leg costume on refrigerators all over town. Speaking of disturbing.

I edged away from the group and went to meet my friends, who were just piling out of Ben's SUV.

"Hey, dude," Ben said, giving me a fist bump.

"Hey, dude," Kirsten said, imitating Ben and also giving me a fist bump.

"Hey," Becca said.

In the sunset orange glow, her hair shimmered all orangey golden as if it had been woven from a real orange and real gold.

"Hey," I replied, suddenly feeling stupidly shy around a girl I had been around lots of times by now and should be well past the point of feeling shy around.

"It was nice of Harley to let us come to his party," Becca said.

"Yeah," I replied. "He's pretty cool."

"Where's the fireworks?" Ben interrupted.

I pointed to a chest-high mound of fireworks piled next to the driveway.

"That should make a pretty good show, don't you think?"

"Whoa," he said, drawn to them like a moth to the proverbial flame. "Let's toss a match into the middle and see what happens."

I gently confiscated the lit match in his hand and blew out the flame.

"There are hot dogs on the grill," I suggested. "And root beer in the cooler."

Ben wandered off, still clutching a box of matches in one hand. Now I understood why Ben's parents didn't keep matches in their house. Or piles of fireworks.

Kirsten followed after him like a parent watching over a curious puppy.

"I'll make sure he doesn't hurt himself," she called back to us.

"He's a funny boy," Becca observed.

"*Funny* isn't the word that usually pops to mind," I clarified.

My train of thought suddenly stopped short as my mother walked out of Harley's house followed by none other than Elsa.

"Stu!" she cried, heading over to us.

Whatever I thought had been going on between Harley and Elsa at the store seemed confirmed by her presence at his party. "Hi, Elsa."

"And I remember you from the day you stopped by the store," Elsa said, addressing Becca. "You must be Becca."

Becca took Elsa's outstretched hand and shook.

"Yes," she replied.

Elsa simply glowed with enthusiasm. "I've heard so much about you."

That seemed like a bit of an exaggeration. The sort of exaggeration bound to set my ears burning. Seriously, are detachable ears too much to ask?

"Hey," Harley said, joining our little group. "Fireworks are about to start. Grab some grub and find a spot to watch the festivities!"

He turned to Elsa. "I've got a couple chairs set up right over here if you'd like to join me to watch the show."

If I didn't know better, I'd swear Harley's ears, what little I could see poking out from his greasy locks, were glowing red-hot. Maybe I wasn't the only one who'd benefit from detachable ears.

"I'd love to!" Elsa gushed.

He guided her over to a couple of lawn chairs set slightly apart from the others.

"Looks like Ben and Kirsten already found a spot," Becca said, pointing.

We found the two of them huddled on a blanket within easy reach of the fireworks pile. Kirsten had positioned herself between Ben and the fireworks, presumably for the safety of others.

The next hour went by in a colorful blur of exploding patriotic mayhem. The rockets' red glare was for real, along with bombs bursting in midair. Everyone under the age of eighty got a chance to light a few fuses along the way and ooh and aah at their own destructive power. Even Ben was entrusted with a handful of matches. He stole the show by twisting the fuses of three rockets together so that he could light them simultaneously with one match.

"You the man," I said as he sat back down.

"More than the man," he snapped back. "The rocket man."

Ben was nothing if not humble.

Becca leaned close. "Do you know where the restroom is?"

"There's one in the house next to the kitchen," I replied. "Or one in the barn next to Harley's workshop."

"Which is closer?" she asked.

"The one in the barn. Want me to show you where it is?"

"Yes, please."

Becca and I slipped through the crowd and across

the gravel driveway to the barn. In the dark, the barn looked a bit like something from a horror movie waiting for two young teens to enter and never be seen again.

"Maybe we should go to the house?" Becca suggested.

I opened the door next to the barn's rolling doors and flipped a light switch. A single bulb flickered an invitation to enter.

"See? Nothing to be frightened of."

Becca stepped through the door.

"I can't see anything."

"Exactly."

I racked my brain to remember the location of the restroom.

"It's next to Harley's workshop," I explained. "Which I'm pretty sure is right over there."

Crossing my fingers, I headed in the general direction of right over there. I didn't get more than a few steps before running into a wall.

"Found it," I groaned, massaging my forehead.

Becca opened the door and flipped on the light.

"Thanks," she said before closing the door behind her.

This left me in a dilemma. Was it better to stand outside the door within earshot of whatever was happening inside? Or retreat back outside and leave Becca alone in Harley's seriously dark and creepy barn? Instead, I groped my way past the restroom until I found the door that led into Harley's workshop. I flipped on the light and stared around in wonder at the contents of the room.

"What is this?" Becca asking, joining me a few moments later.

A dizzying variety of sculptures made from old barn wood, barbed wire, barn windows, rope, and miscellaneous pieces of rusted metal filled the room. "This is Harley's art studio."

Becca walked to the center of the room, then turned in a circle taking it all in.

"I didn't know he was an artist."

"Yeah, he uses reclaimed materials he gets from old barns and stuff. My dad says it's tough to make a living as an artist, but Harley is starting to sell pieces to people as far away as Montana and Colorado."

"Wow, that's so cool!"

"Yeah, checking out his workshop is my favorite part about coming here."

She delicately touched one of the sculptures with a finger.

"I can see why. It's like the past and the present are all jumbled together in cool ways."

I pointed to one that had a rubber duck peeking out through the glass pane of an old window. "Some of them are pretty funny, too. My mom calls his art 'Whimsical Repurposed Americana.'"

Becca stood next to a sculpture of a woman with her hands on her hips made completely out of rusted barbed wire.

"Who's that?"

"Oh, that's Barb. Harley says it's a likeness of his first girlfriend. I guess she had a sharp temper."

Becca giggled. "You weren't kidding about his sense of humor."

"That's what's so great about him. He's all easygoing

and cool, but then you see his artwork and there's this whole other side to him."

Becca turned to face me. "You really like Harley, don't you?"

My head nodded involuntarily. "Yeah, people see him and think he's some greasy biker dude. But really, he's a super-nice guy when you get to know him. I kinda wish I was more like him."

She floated across the room until she was standing right in front of me.

"You're pretty cool in your own way," she said in a soft voice that made my skin tingle.

"Really?"

She leaned close, her eyes as blue and fathomless as my favorite Lego blocks.

"Yes," she whispered.

My lips puckered against my will. Whatever was happening I was powerless to stop it. I leaned forward, the unimaginable about to happen.

"Whatcha doin'?"

Ben and Kirsten stood in the doorway.

"Wha—no—nothin—" Becca and I stammered.

Ben and Kirsten's eyes suddenly went wide like they'd seen a ghost, or their closest friends about to kiss.

"Oh, sorry," Kirsten said.

"Dude," Ben added, his eyes shouting *You the man* at me.

"We were just looking for you to let you know the fireworks had ended," Kirsten said in a rush, pulling Ben back out the door.

Maybe the fireworks outside had ended. The fireworks inside never quite got started. I wasn't sure whether to hug them in thanks or hang Ben from Barb's armpit.

"I guess we should go back before your parents wonder where we are," Becca said.

"Yeah, I guess so."

I stared up at the stars on the way home and wondered how my life had gotten so complicated. Just months ago, I was happy being a guy who still built fortresses out of Legos without girls or a care in the world.

What had happened to me? Now I couldn't even

enjoy a quiet night of exploding fireworks without facing the risk of another sort of fireworks going off. I missed the old days. But I couldn't go back. My world had become more dangerous, more unpredictable, and more real than ever before. And somehow more intriguing, too. Sometimes I kinda even liked it. Sometimes.

The next day at work, Elsa was bubblier than ever. She nearly shrieked when I entered the store.

"Stu! I'm so glad to see you! After everyone left last night, Harley and I stayed up and planned out the entire fashion show."

She opened a notebook filled with notes and diagrams that looked like some sort of secret battle plans intended to win the war to end all wars.

"Harley is so creative," she enthused. "Look at how he diagrammed the store and how we can set up for the show this year. The catwalk is going to run right through the middle of the store with chairs on either side just like a real fashion show."

She grabbed her purse and jammed the notebook inside.

"I'm off to meet with the rental folks who are providing the risers, chairs, curtains, tables, and everything else we need." She twirled on her way out like a toddler in a toy store. "This is going to be the best show ever!"

After the windstorm known as Elsa left, things were a lot quieter. That left me time to sweep the floors, tidy up behind the counter, and sprinkle sparkly confetti about the store. Not really. Mostly, I sat hunched over on the stool behind the counter and tried not to fall asleep. About the time my eyelids closed for good, the front door burst open and a gaggle of ladies led by Diane marched into the store.

"Stu!" Diane said. "I'm so glad you're here. I was just telling the ladies that with luck you would be here to help us take advantage of the twenty-five-percent-off coupon that we all received in the mail the other day."

Lucky me.

"What can I help you with?"

A lady with silver hair and penciled black eyebrows stepped forward.

"What do you have in the way of swimwear?" she asked.

Swimwear? I wasn't comfortable being seen in my own swim trunks, let alone helping a group of senior citizens find bikinis.

"Um . . . I'm not sure."

"Mildred, you just follow me," Diane said, leading the way to the back corner. "I'll get you started while Stu helps Audrey."

A frail woman with white hair sidled up to the counter.

"I need a new handbag."

She held hers up so I could see that the clasp had broken.

"I haven't had a new handbag in years."

"They're right over here," I directed, pointing to a table right next to her.

"Oh, aren't they lovely?" she asked.

She lifted the closest one and inspected it inside and out.

"Do you have something like this but in navy blue?"

I picked up the purse next to the one she was holding.

"Do you mean like this one?"

"Oh, yes," she replied. She patted the handle. "I used

to work at Macy's a long time ago. I dreamed of having a navy-blue hand-sewn leather handbag with gold snaps just like all the rich ladies had." She stroked the faux leather. "But then I got married and had four beautiful children and I never once missed owning such a gaudy extravagance." She gazed down at the handbag rocking in her arms like an infant. "Okay, maybe I missed it a little bit."

She handed me the bag and headed for the cash register.

"But now my kids are grown, my husband is long since deceased, my investments are holding steady, and I have this here coupon. So, at long last, I'm going to get the bag I always dreamed of having."

She paid and then rejoined Diane and the other ladies.

"Look what that fine young man found for me," she said, showing off her new handbag.

"It's beautiful," Diane agreed. "I told you he was the darling who would hook you up with whatever you needed."

According to Diane, I had some sort of supernatural

powers when it came to helping ladies with their fashion needs. Nothing could have been further from the truth. But what good did it do to argue? They'd only find me humble as well as talented.

Diane waved me over. Next to her stood a little woman with short cropped black hair and the smallest hands I'd ever seen that didn't belong to my little brother.

"Honey, this is Aiko. She and her husband recently moved here from Southern California and joined our ballroom dance group."

Diane put an arm around the little woman.

"She sure knows her way around the dance floor."

Aiko gave a little bow with her head.

"She only says that because I make her sushi on Tuesdays."

"But she's got a problem," Diane continued. "She needs a dress that says 'watch me,' don't you, Aiko?"

Aiko blushed but didn't refuse the notion.

"Perhaps something teal green," she said.

I followed Aiko as she browsed rack to rack ignoring the green dresses in favor of the red ones.

"My mother always said I looked good in teal," she confided. "But I always preferred red."

"I had to wear pink last week," I confided in return. "I didn't even know they made pink shirts for men."

She held out a sparkly red dress for inspection.

"I bet you looked very handsome in pink."

Pretty sure I had looked foolish. "I don't know. Maybe."

She carried the dress to a dressing room and disappeared inside. A few minutes later, she pirouetted from the dressing room looking all jangly and glowing in the red dress.

"You go, girl!" Diane shouted from across the store.

Aiko blushed as she admired herself in a mirror.

"Yes, I will take it," she confirmed.

Diane waved me back over to the bathing suit area.

"Well, what do you think?" she asked.

Mildred held a one-piece bathing suit up to herself in front of a mirror on the wall.

What did I think? Well, I loved the way the bathing suit was still on the hanger and not being modeled for real. "Looks good."

"If Stu approves, then you're all good to go," Diane said.

"Yes, it looks good," Mildred repeated, "for a woman of my advanced years. I think I can swim laps in this thing all right."

The ladies paid at the register, and then Diane swept them for the door.

"Time for a late lunch, girls," she called.

The door swung shut with a happy clang as they made their way next door to the Sunshine Café.

Elsa returned just before two.

"I got it all lined up," she said, beaming. "It's going to be perfect. Just perfect. Thanks for all your help."

What exactly had I done? "Sure."

22

That evening Ben and I popped a couple root beers, sat back, and reflected on our start to the summer.

"We're a couple of working stiffs," Ben said, taking a big swig from the can in his hand. "Like, how did that happen?"

"Well, for you I think it had a lot to do with not turning in your homework all year."

"Yeah, but if I'd done that, I'd be sleeping in and playing *Death Intruders* every day instead of 'learning quality life lessons out in the real world.'" Ben quoted the last part in his father's voice.

"I get you being punished, but I didn't even do anything wrong," I complained.

"Your grandmother's out to get you."

"Yeah, that's what I keep thinking."

"She'll do anything to force you into wearing pink and waiting on little old ladies."

"Yeah, she's cruel that way."

"And cunning. Who else could pull off such a dastardly evil plan?"

"Seriously, who thinks to break their hip in order to make their grandson suffer?"

"Genius, when you think about it."

"Yep, my grandmother's a diabolical genius."

After a quick hour of *Death Intruders*, I said good night and headed home. The sugar buzz had me in high spirits, that and having thoroughly spanked Ben at zombie football. The two combined to make the first half block of my walk pure pleasure. That is, right up until the world tilted. Jackson stood leaning against one of the columns on Becca's porch, his lone chin hair gleaming in the moonlight.

"See you tomorrow," he said to the figure in the doorway.

The sight stopped me cold. What was he doing there? Maybe it was the root beer talking, but I had the sudden urge to throw that no-good, bicep-flexing poser off the steps. If only the zombie warlord in my chest would stop flailing about like an undead petulant baby.

Instead, I ducked low and ran. Sure, there might have been more mature ways to handle the situation. Like joining them on the porch. Or sucker-punching Jackson when he wasn't looking. But none of those ideas ran through my head until after I slammed the door shut to my room and buried my head under my pillow.

Last night in Harley's barn returned to mind. Had I misunderstood the moment? Had she really been about to kiss me? Or had I imagined the look in her eyes? What if I'd imagined everything? What if she's never seen me as more than a friend? What if it's all been made-up fantasies like my nightly rescues in the woods? Or, worse yet, what if she had liked me but not anymore?

When I thought about it, I had lied to her all spring. And spurted blood all over her at the square-dancing assembly. And made a fool of myself in front of everyone on my father's float. And, to top it off, the moment she leaned in for a kiss, I hesitated just long enough for the whole thing to be ruined. No wonder she wanted someone smarter, and studlier, and with infinitely more chin hair.

Maybe I shouldn't feel too bad. Ryan and Tyler hadn't lasted two weeks before they got dumped. Depending on how you figured it, Becca and I had gone out twice as long before she got wise and found a bigger, better, more normal boyfriend.

Strangely, that didn't make me feel better. All that really mattered was that Jackson had been standing on her porch while I stood below unseen and unwanted.

Figured.

**23**

I hid my feelings over the next few days by focusing on work. Not really.

"Stu, is something the matter?" Elsa asked for the umpteenth time.

I sulkily stared down at the unfolded blouse in my hands. "No."

One thing I'd discovered is that the art of sulking takes practice. It had taken over a week for me to reach the point where I could hold a blouse for hours and still not find the willpower to fold it.

"Stu," Elsa said, guiding me away from the pile of unfolded garments. "Let's talk. What's up?"

It would ruin the whole sulking thing to actually talk to someone.

"Is this about Becca?" she prodded.

No, of course not. I couldn't possibly be feeling this crummy just because of a girl. "Maybe."

"Did you guys have a fight?"

I wished. A fight would have only involved the two of us, not that flexing poser Jackson. "No, not exactly." I dug deep for the courage to say what needed to be said. "I think she likes someone else."

A tiny gasp caught in Elsa's throat. I had been having similar gasps lately every time I took a breath.

"Oh, I see."

She looked around as if to make sure we weren't being spied on.

"What makes you say that?"

Now that it was out in the open, I couldn't stop myself from telling her about that muscle-bloated party crasher Jackson. I ended the story with what I'd seen and heard walking home from Ben's house.

Elsa's head bobbed up and down as she thought.

"Sometimes when we care about someone it's easy to jump to a wrong conclusion. Have you talked to her?"

What sort of crazy advice was that? Did Elsa actually think I should sit down with Becca, tell her what I'd seen, and ask for an explanation? Sure, that seemed reasonable. But if I asked, she might respond. And I wasn't ready to hear the answer.

Two p.m. rolled around and I shuffled out the front door still wrapped in my cloak of sulkiness. I should have known better than to talk to an adult. All Elsa had done was leave me feeling more unsure about things than ever. Talk to Becca about my concerns? Seriously, who did that? She made it sound so simple, but when was the last time she had talked out an issue with anyone?

I stepped into the sunlight, and there stood Becca waiting for me on the sidewalk.

"Hi," she said.

My cloak fell to the ground, leaving me exposed in my own uncomfortable skin. "Hi."

She headed away from the store, and I followed like the obedient puppy dog I had become.

"I had to take care of my sister all morning while my mom was at a doctor's appointment. Carly's the worst. Want to get some ice cream?"

There was probably something important I needed

to be doing, like running away, but my mind had gone totally blank. "Sure."

Becca reached up as if to touch the sunlight as we walked.

"The weather here is so beautiful in the summer," she said. "We used to live in LA, and it would be so hot we couldn't even go outside sometimes."

"Wow, I've never really thought about what it's like in other places. I'd die in that kind of heat."

"Yeah," she giggled. "Sometimes I thought I'd melt."

We reached the ice cream shop and entered. All the same flavors of ice cream beckoned from inside the glass case. I went with my old standby, chocolate chocolate-chip, while Becca agonized over whether vanilla was better paired with a caramel or raspberry swirl.

"It's so hard to choose," she said.

I taste tested the two tubs of ice cream fueling her debate.

"Not for me. Just get a scoop of each and call it good."

"Perfect," she agreed.

We sat on the curb in front of the store and went to work dismantling our heaping cones of frozen goodness.

"How is working at your grandmother's store going?" she asked.

Up until the last few days, it had seemed pretty much fine. The sulking had kinda gotten in the way recently. Speaking of sulking, this seemed like a perfect time to follow Elsa's advice and get things out on the table. "It's okay." Maybe I could have been a little more forthright in bringing up my concerns. "I pretty much know all there is to know about pantsuits."

She smiled. "That sounds important."

"Yeah, Elsa is thinking of promoting me to pantsuit accessories manager next."

"What sort of accessories do pantsuits need?"

"A heavy gold chain and diamond-rimmed reading glasses always look good."

"Or maybe a plaid handbag?"

"Absolutely! Hey, maybe you can get a job at the store as the plaid handbag sales consultant?"

"That sounds perfect!"

By this point I had forgotten all about the other night and that half man Jackson. Which was okay by me. In a choice between awkward discussions and playful banter, the choice seemed easy. "The sundries department is also looking for help."

"I wouldn't want to keep you from helping little old ladies with their sundries needs."

"True. No one knows sundries like I do."

**24**

Spending the afternoon with Becca had a remarkable way of lifting me out of my sulky doom and gloom. The chocolate chocolate-chip didn't hurt, either. Elsa noticed my change of mood the next morning and took full advantage of it.

"Stu! All the details for the show are coming together. We just need to pick out the fashions."

She pulled out a catalog about the size of my house and began thumbing through it.

"What do you think of this?" she asked, pointing to an all-too-skinny model wearing something that looked like the rug in our living room.

"Uh, I guess so."

"Or how about this?" she said, pointing to a woman

with a poodle hairdo wearing a shawl that could've passed for our bath mat.

Had someone been designing women's clothing based on the thrift store furnishings in the Truly household? The idea seemed impossible but so did the idea of a woman in a catalog wearing a fuzzy pink bath mat. "I guess."

Elsa flipped page by page through the catalog marking roughly half the items as possibilities.

"Thanks. You were such a help!" she said after we had finished. "We can narrow it down further tomorrow."

An internal groan escaped my lips.

"What was that?"

"I said I can hardly wait."

Elsa gave me a conspiratorial grin.

"With you, me, and Harley working together, this show is going to be great!"

Yeah, probably bath-mat great. Maybe even living-room-rug great. Probably so great my grandmother will ban me from ever setting foot in her store again.

The next day, the process of narrowing down our

fashion show choices continued. In fact, the next week mostly consisted of watching Elsa fawn over all the choices in the catalog. Fortunately, we had help. Diane and company stopped by daily to get a sneak peek and weigh in on their choices for the show.

"Do you think we should leave out the poodle skirt with the poodle tail in back?" Elsa asked the group.

"Absolutely not," Diane countered. "What could be cuter paired with the purple polka-dot cashmere sweater?"

"Oh yes," Mildred agreed. "Especially if it's followed by the high-waisted sailor slacks with side buckles."

"Don't forget the crimson evening gown," Aiko added.

Elsa rubbed her temples. "There are just so many perfect choices. I wish we could order them all."

Given that we'd been having the same discussion for five days straight, I just wished someone would make a decision and put an end to the misery.

After the ladies left to get lunch, Elsa slumped down against the counter.

"How am I ever going to finalize the show if I

can't decide on what to order?"

That seemed like an excellent question. Personally, I grabbed whatever looked clean in my laundry basket and ran with it.

"You're right," she replied, as if reading my mind. "I need to trust my instincts."

Say what?

"And get this order finalized so the items arrive in time. And stop fixating on little details and have faith that everything is going to work out fine. And stop worrying about whether Rosemarie would approve."

Whoa, apparently a lot of important thoughts had been running through my mind. Glad at least one of us noticed.

"Thanks, Stu, for getting me back on track."

Elsa got on the computer and went to work placing the order. Meanwhile, I took a seat at the counter and rested my aching head. Telepathic communication wears a guy out.

On my way home, I ran into Harley. I didn't recognize him at first due to the way he was holding a bouquet of flowers and a box of chocolates out in front of him as if they were explosives poised to go off. At the sight of me, he stopped short.

"Hey, Stu," he said, staring down awkwardly at the gifts in each hand.

"Hey, Harley. Where you going?"

Watching a grown man's ears heat up to burning hot is humbling. For them.

"Being as how I just happened to be in town and all—I thought I'd stop in for a moment"—beads of sweat rolled down his forehead, which seemed strange since it was only a seventy-degree day—"and say hi to Elsa."

Something about his statement didn't quite add up, maybe it was the flowers and chocolates sparkling in the sunlight. He lowered his voice.

"Do you think flowers and chocolates are too much?"

Not if he was planning to propose to her. HE WASN'T PLANNING TO PROPOSE TO HER, WAS HE?

"Uh . . . no . . . I'm sure she'll like them."

Unless they're hiding a ring with a lifetime commitment attached. I was pretty sure she wasn't ready for that.

"We've been spending time together for three weeks now," he explained.

So, the chocolates and flowers were to celebrate their three-week-spending-time-together anniversary? Harley was more smitten than I thought. "Come to think of it, I think she's sworn off sweets for the summer. Maybe just the flowers would be best for now."

Alarm flashed across Harley's face.

"Oh, thanks, man. I didn't know. I'm not so good at this sort of thing."

That's for darn sure.

He jammed the chocolates into his jacket pocket.

"You saved me."

Poor guy. When you're blushing in front of thirteen-year-olds, you're beyond saving.

25

Seeing Harley looking all love-addled got me thinking. Maybe that's what women look for in a guy. If so, Becca must find me the most attractive guy on earth. The idea made total sense so long as I didn't think about it too much.

After I got home, I pulled out my pen and notebook. If Harley wasn't afraid to embarrass himself publicly, then the least I could do was finish the poem I never really started for Becca's birthday. I curled up on my bed and got to work. Strange, the blank page seemed to have grown since my last attempt. And my pen had shrunk to the size of a sewing needle. How was I supposed to fill such a huge space with a writing utensil so small?

Pushing my doubts aside, I wrote the first thing that came to mind.

*Your face is better than birthday cake,*
*round and sweet and nice.*
*Like unchewed bubble gum*
*or grape-flavored shaved ice.*

A gag crept up my throat. Her face is better than birthday cake? What did that mean? Like unchewed bubble gum? The gag made room for a second, larger gag. Or grape-flavored shaved ice? A full-on heave clenched my gut. The page went into the garbage can at the foot of my bed. I wanted to impress her, not make her physically ill.

The next hour continued the process of poetic musings followed by gut-wrenching heaves that left me with a sore stomach and a garbage can full of crumpled pages. Reluctantly, I returned to the roses-are-red approach.

*Roses are red*
*and violets are blue.*
*Something something something*
*I love you.*

I simply needed to replace the *something something something* with something that actually made sense. And the *I love you* with something other than *I love you* because those words weren't happening in my first-ever birthday poem for a girl I wasn't sure I was actually going out with.

By dinnertime, I had stared at the words *something something something* until I started to accept their reality. She really was something something something, wasn't she? My hand gave the customary slap to the forehead. Of course, she was something, but what? I didn't have a clue.

That night at dinner, my mother seemed full of questions I had no interest in answering.

"So, Stu, how is your work at the store coming along?"

"Okay."

"Are you learning a lot?"

"I guess."

"Elsa a good boss?"

"Sure."

She frowned. "You're not exactly being forthcoming. Has it really been that bad?"

Well, let's see. So far, I had touched an old woman's back while zipping up her dress, worn a pink polo shirt in public, sprinkled sparkly sprinkles about the store, and discussed the merits of purple polka-dot sweaters with a group of women roughly five times my age. All in all, it had been a real hoot. "I'm working at an old ladies' clothing store. What do you think?"

My mother carved another slab from the pot roast and plunked it on my plate.

"How about the fashion show? Is it happening this year?"

"Harley told me he's been helping her design the layout for the show," my father added between mouthfuls of potatoes.

He gave my mom a wink.

"He seems more than willing to give Elsa any help she needs."

My mother hid her smile behind her hand.

"Now you leave those two alone. The last thing they need is people jumping to conclusions and spreading gossip around town."

"Do you mean like how Harley brought her flowers this afternoon?"

My mother choked on her roll. "He brought her flowers?"

"He said it had been three weeks since they started spending time together."

My father set down his fork, a grim look replacing the mischievous gleam in his eye. "I told him not to rush things and take it slow. He always gets so wound up it scares the poor woman half to death. He didn't propose, did he?"

Exactly what I had been wondering. "I don't know. I don't think so. I was leaving the store when I ran into him."

"I'm sure everything is all right," my mother interjected. "I'm sure he learned from last time."

My father lifted his fork, then set it back down.

"I better talk to him tomorrow. I'm sure you're right. But just in case . . ."

From the look I had seen on Harley's face earlier, my father had better talk to him soon.

26

The next day after work, I headed over to the school soccer field. I found the guys waiting for me to get in a little unofficial practice before our team's official practices started up in August. Mostly it gave us an excuse to hang out and shoot the breeze without anyone's parents complaining that we were spending our summer inside in front of a video game console rather than out getting some fresh air.

"Hey, you made it!" Ben shouted.

He blistered a shot that missed my backside by inches. My fault for veering in front of the goal.

"I see you still can't hit the goalie—let alone the goal," I shouted back.

A second shot whizzed past my ear into the upper corner of the net. Tyler gave me a thumbs-up.

"At least I still got it."

I checked my face for windburn. Geez, that dude had a rocket leg.

"Yep, that's why I don't play goalie."

Ryan gave Tyler a shove.

"How'd you get it to curve right for his head?"

"Easy, I pictured him square-dancing with Gretchen and the ball curved on its own."

I dribbled the ball out of the net and zipped it across the turf.

"Are you telling me you had an assassin ball in your possession this spring, but kept it secret? The least you could have done was kill us all during square dancing and put us out of our misery."

Tyler redirected the pass to Ben.

"And keep you from being properly socialized? Are you kidding? I'd never be so cruel."

Ben smashed the ball to Ryan, who redirected it my direction.

"No more talk about Gretchen."

"Ryan's still mad," Tyler explained. "She's already going out with someone else from her church."

"How do you know that?" Ben asked.

Tyler popped the ball up in the air, then juggled it with his knees.

"We go to the same church. It happened at camp last week."

Ryan stole the ball from Tyler and sent it skimming over to Ben.

"That's not all that happened at camp," Ryan goaded.

Ben stopped the ball with one foot and held it there.

"Wait, what else happened?"

"He kissed a girl he met."

"What?" Ben and I shouted together.

Tyler shrugged his shoulders like it was nothing, but the grin on his face had grown to the size of Ben's head.

"We kinda snuck off and went for a walk. And then she just sort of kissed me."

Just sort of kissed him? How does something like that just happen?

"What do you mean she kissed you?" Ben prompted.

Tyler's sheepish shrug gave way to a haughty look of manly superiority, the sort of look I could only imagine giving should I ever cross into the land of the casually kissed. Though by then my friends would be living in an old folks' home, too nearsighted to notice.

"Well, she took my face in her hands and then kissed me."

That brought all the giggling to a halt. The image of a girl putting her hands on Tyler's face was more than I could handle. I had thrown water balloons at that face. Ben had written *dork* on that face while Tyler had been sleeping. Just this spring, future cover-model Annie had kissed that face—wha? The thought made me stagger. He had kissed two girls? What was the world coming to?

A moment of silence ensued. Not to memorialize Tyler's accomplishment. No one could think of anything to say after his bomb-dropping revelation. Further questioning seemed pointless. He had risen to another plane. One that involved girlish hands, boyish cheeks, and two sets of lips locked in an epic struggle for singularity. How were we to comprehend that?

Soccer suddenly seemed like a vital connection to the past. Something to renew our bonds as friends in a time of barbaric unrest. An act of solidarity to hold at bay the enemy hoards at the gates, who even now were trying to tear apart our friendship one lip-gloss moment at a time.

Two hours later, my pits were sweaty, my legs tired, and my brain exhausted from trying to understand how two of my oldest friends had gone from comic books and lightsaber duels to lip-locking with girls in the blink of a single summer.

"Hey, you guys want to hike down to the Spit tomorrow?" Tyler asked.

The Dungeness Spit is a strip of land that runs for miles out into the Strait of Juan de Fuca just outside town. It's pretty much the coolest place on earth to build driftwood forts.

Ben and I shared a helpless look.

"I gotta work at my dad's store tomorrow," Ben growled. "He's making a man of me. And slowly destroying my will to live."

"Me too," I added.

"Can't you skip one day?" Tyler pressed.

"Not unless I want to be locked in the storeroom for

the rest of my life," Ben explained.

"Or I want to be guilted by my parents about my grandmother's broken hip," I added.

Tyler chipped the ball over to me. "Wow, that blows."

My last shot on goal skimmed under Ben's foot into the back of the net. "Yeah, I gotta go home and get back to sulking. Otherwise, my parents might start to think I'm enjoying working there."

"Yeah, my mom is picking Tyler and me up in the parking lot," Ryan agreed. "I got a piano lesson tonight."

"His piano creeps me out," Ben said as we walked across the field together toward home. "I think it's possessed."

Ryan's mom bought a baby grand just so he could take piano lessons. It growls every time someone walks past. Ryan says it's the vibrations from our feet making the bass strings vibrate. But I'm pretty sure the piano is crazy jealous of anything that disrupts Ryan's practice time.

"Me too. Probably came from a funeral home."

"Yeah, they probably sold it because undead customers kept eating the pianist."

"That'd be the coolest funeral ever if you had to hide to keep from being eaten by the person you came to mourn."

"Especially if you had to hide inside the funeral home, like in caskets and stuff."

"Why doesn't *Death Intruders* have a level like that?"

"Seriously, they're missing out." Ben swept his hands as if showing off a marketing poster. "*Death Intruders 5*: Funeral Fun for the Whole Family."

"Who wouldn't want to play a game where you're chased by your own dead relatives?"

Ben shrugged his shoulders. "Beats me."

We left the soccer field and followed a sidewalk that led past the elementary school playground. The warm afternoon had brought loads of parents to watch their kids climb on the jungle gym, swing on the swings, and dig in the giant sand box. A few of the adults I recognized from school events. Some had older kids close to my age. On the far side of the playground stood a young couple with two little girls running around them playing tag. The young couple looked oddly familiar.

"Hey, isn't that Becca?" Ben asked. "With Jackson?"

27

I froze midstep. What were they doing together? The image of Jackson on Becca's porch the other night flashed to mind. I should've plucked that chin hair when I had the chance. Could there really be something going on between them? First, they square-dance together in PE. Then they slow-dance together at the school dance. Then they ride on his church's parade float in the festival parade. And now they were on the playground looking like a newly married couple. When I thought about it, Jackson had spent a lot more time with Becca than I had.

As if to prove my point, she looked up at him and laughed, as if even his jokes were funnier. My stomach flipped over, climbed up my throat, and slapped my face from the inside.

"C'mon," I said. "Let's get out of here before they see us."

"Don't you want to go over there and say hi?"

Ben could be such a naive idiot. "No, let's get out of here."

My eyes stayed on the sidewalk until we got to Ben's house.

"What's going on?" he asked once we were safely inside.

"She dumped me for Jackson."

"What?"

"Didn't you see the way she was looking at him? And how he stood there looking all fatherly like they were discussing what to name their next child?"

Ben led me to the fridge and got out two ice-cold root beers.

"You might be overreacting a little bit. They were just standing on the playground talking."

"They were more than talking."

I tossed back a swig of the dark brew. Fizzing bubbles burned my throat as the sweet syrup slid down. Before long, I'd be lost in a sugar stupor. And then maybe I could forget, at least for a little while.

"They were just standing there."

"I saw Jackson on Becca's porch the other night."

Ben set his bottle down on the counter.

"Hang on. What do you mean you saw Jackson on Becca's porch? You didn't tell me that."

"What was I supposed to do? Call you up and say, 'Hey, Ben, thought you should know Jackson that giant gum wad is currently hanging out on Becca's porch'?"

"Yeah, that would've worked."

I lowered my root beer. Even with ice cream it'd never give me a sugar buzz big enough to forget what I'd seen. "Well, I didn't, so shut up."

"It was probably nothing."

"It was probably everything."

"I'll ask Kirsten."

"NO!"

The last thing I needed was for Ben to go blabbering to his girlfriend about me being all paranoid. She'd tell Becca and then Becca would— What would Becca do? Confirm the rumor? Deny it? It didn't matter. I knew what I'd seen with my own eyes. Why make things worse by triggering a chain of gossip bound to embarrass me even more? It was over, and I needed to face the truth of it.

"Promise me you won't say anything to Kirsten."

"Okay, okay, take it easy."

Yeah, right. You take it easy.

The short walk home took forever. Mostly because my feet sunk into the sidewalk as I neared Becca's house. What if they were inside? What if they saw me walking past and decided it was the perfect moment to announce their engagement? What if evil death monkeys fell from the sky, took me hostage, and forced me to watch the two of them holding hands by a crackling fire while sipping sparkling cider from matching crystal champagne glasses?

No, I had not gone completely bat-poop crazy. Okay, yes, the zombie warlord had curled into the fetal position refusing to acknowledge me. And yes, a single tear may have gone rogue and made a mad dash for my chin. But, no, I had not gone crazy.

And that's when Becca's father opened the front door and stepped out onto the porch. No, he didn't notice me. Except that he did. For a long moment, he stood and stared at the teary, mumbling crazy kid below on the sidewalk.

"She's not here," he said at last.

And then he turned and went back inside.

Speaking of evil death monkeys.

28

I arrived at work the next morning feeling about as awful as you'd expect after a fitful night of haunted dreams involving a werewolf, a chin-haired creature from the deep, and a fair-haired mermaid as lovely as she was cruel. In each nightmare, the fair-haired mermaid would call from somewhere far out at sea. I'd give in to the call and row out in a leaky rowboat only to discover a grumpy werewolf had joined me on the adventure. Every time the mermaid rose to the surface in greeting, the werewolf would howl, and then the creature from the deep would surface, grab one of the oars, and use it to bash the rowboat to smithereens. Then the three of them would swim off together, leaving me clinging to a chunk of waterlogged wood. Sweet dreams.

The only saving grace was knowing Elsa would be

waiting to console me. She had become like a big sister in the last few weeks. Someone I could talk to about things in a way I couldn't with my parents or friends. Someone I could count on when times were tough. Someone who could bring the perspective I desperately needed, or at least a shoulder to lean on.

"AHH, EVERYTHING'S RUINED!" Elsa wailed the moment I entered.

So much for a shoulder to lean on.

"What's ruined?"

She stumbled from behind the counter, her eyes wild.

"EVERYTHING! IT'S ALL MY FAULT!"

Her hands alternated between covering her eyes and clenching into fists.

"I'M SUCH AN IDIOT, IDIOT, IDIOT! YOUR GRANDMOTHER'S GOING TO KILL ME!"

By this point, I was totally confused and a tad bit frightened. I had seen people get upset, just yesterday I'd been a bit upset myself. But I'd never seen an adult have a complete meltdown. I approached her with my hands out in front of me like the park ranger in

167

a documentary I once saw approaching a frightened wildebeest.

"Elsa, take it easy," I tried.

She slumped back against the counter. Her outburst calmed to racking sobs.

"I'm such an idiot," she moaned. "Such a stupid freaking idiot."

Wow, and I thought I could be hard on myself. Cautiously, I sidled up next to the counter close enough to show support, but far enough away to stay outside her reach.

"Elsa, what happened?"

"This is what happened," she said, pressing the play button on the store's answering machine.

*Hi, Elsa. This is Brittany from Northwest Models. Thanks for your message last night. I'm sorry to say we'll be unable to provide the models for your show this year. We never got the signed contract back, and our models are now booked for other events that weekend. Best of luck to you with the show. Hope we can work together again next year. Bye.*

Elsa pulled out a document from a folder labeled Fall Fashion Show and plopped it on the counter.

"This is the contract they sent the day your grandmother broke her hip. I was supposed to sign it and send it back."

She sniffled, dabbing at both eyes.

"But I was upset about your grandmother, and then I got caught up in all the other preparations."

The sniffling turned to more sobs.

"And then Harley showed up, and asked me to his Fourth of July party, and then he brought me flowers, and I got all distracted and forgot to sign the contract and send it back. And now it's too late, and the show is ruined, and it's all my fault."

I wanted to tell her at least there wasn't a grumpy werewolf haunting her dreams, but it didn't seem like the time. "Are there other models you can get?"

She blew her nose and tossed the tissue onto the growing mountain of other tissues in the garbage.

"That's all I've been doing since I got here. I've tried every modeling agency in the Seattle area. To them our little show is a joke. Only one would even give me a price, and it was outrageous. The store doesn't have that kind of money. The show only happens because your grandmother and the owner of Northwest Models have been friends forever. She gives us a deal as a favor to support a local, woman-owned business. But I messed up and now everything's ruined!"

More sobbing ensued. I went so far as to pat her shoulder. A hug probably would have been appropriate, but I couldn't bring myself to be that adultlike. The door opened, and Diane sauntered in wearing her sky-blue sweater and sporting a smile filled with summer-time cheer.

"How are my two favorite fashionistas?"

The sobbing fountain formerly known as Elsa gave a weak wave. Diane stopped short.

"Hang on a minute. What's going on here?"

She gave me a hip check that sent me sliding out of the way, then wrapped her arm around Elsa's shoulders.

"Does he have another girlfriend?"

"No."

"Involved in drugs?"

"No."

"Doesn't want a serious relationship?"

Elsa dabbed at her eyes again.

"It's not about Harley."

"Oh. Your mom?"

"No."

Diane turned her attention to me.

"I'm out of ideas. What's going on here?"

"There's a problem with the modeling agency for the fashion show," I explained. "They can't come this year."

"Because I messed up," Elsa blurted. "It's all my fault, and now the show is ruined."

Diane handed Elsa a tissue. "Oh, I see. Well, at least no one died or had their heart broken."

Elsa grunted. "This is what happens when I get involved with a man. My brain stops working right, and something bad happens. I should have known better than to let my feelings get in the way of my work."

Somehow that didn't seem like an accurate depiction of what had gone down. Diane let out a laugh.

"Honey, a man is like a sack of potatoes. Best kept in the cellar until you're ready to toss 'em on the skillet, if you know what I mean."

That brought a giggle from Elsa for reasons no one seemed willing to explain.

"When you gonna break the news to Rosemarie?" Diane asked.

More tissues were called in to mop up the latest plumbing leak in Elsa's face. At last she took a deep breath.

"As soon as I find the courage."

Diane gave her shoulders another squeeze.

"Take your time, honey. Take your time."

29

I got home that afternoon to find my mother busy in the kitchen packing a cooler.

"Stu, your grandmother got out of the nursing home today. Your dad and I just got her settled in at her house. I'm putting together some frozen meals for her."

She handed me the cooler. It weighed more than my little brother.

"I need you to take this cooler to her so I can get back to work. And I think she'd appreciate a visit."

Had my mother seen my biceps?

"I can't carry this all the way to her house. It weighs like five hundred pounds."

She sized me up with one of her famous where-did-I-go-wrong-as-a-parent? eye rolls.

"Five hundred pounds is a bit of an exaggeration.

You can use Tommy's wagon if you like."

Seriously? She expected me to drag my little brother's red wagon across town?

"Can't you just drive me there?"

"No."

Negotiating with my parents is the worst. I ate a quick snack and then hitched myself to the wagon like a compliant ox heading out on the Oregon Trail. Actually, I pretty much just grabbed the handle with one hand and started pulling.

"Have a safe trip," my mother called as I plodded down the driveway.

The slow journey to my grandmother's house gave me time to contemplate whose life was more miserable: Elsa's or mine. Elsa had just made arguably the worst mistake of her life. One that might send my grandmother's store into a tailspin. I, on the other hand, was grinding my teeth away to the gums after realizing that the girl I liked was going out with the boy whose chin hair I hated most. So, which was worse? Being publicly ridiculed for ruining an annual tradition? Or being forced to watch Jackson and Becca laugh at each other's jokes? The winner seemed obvious.

About time the beads of sweat dripping off my forehead permanently blurred my vision, I pulled into my grandmother's driveway and parked my brother's cruddy wagon on the front lawn. The cooler banged against the door as I pushed it open.

"Hi, Grandma!" I called.

"I'm in the kitchen!" she called back.

I found her whipping up a peanut butter sandwich.

"Finally, I can make a meal for myself," she commented.

The cooler thunked on the linoleum.

"Mom had me bring some meals for you to put in your freezer," I explained.

"That's very kind of her," she replied. "Though I told her I can get around just fine to make meals for myself now."

She went to work unloading the cooler into the freezer. Compared to the last time I saw her, she looked good as new.

"Your hip doing better?"

She patted it with one hand.

"Still sore as the dickens. But I'm moving around pretty well now. And the doctor says it will only get better over the next few weeks."

She poured two cups of lemonade and motioned for us to sit on the couch in the living room. Watching her ease onto the couch made it clear that her recovery still had a ways to go.

"Well," she said, taking a sip of her lemonade. "What's new with you?"

Well, let's see. My personal life was in shambles. A grumpy werewolf haunted my dreams. And I had just watched Elsa have a total breakdown at the store. "Not much."

"Is that right. Then why is your leg twitching?"

Her broken hip hadn't injured her vision. "I'm okay, really."

She set her lemonade on the coffee table.

"You're really a terrible liar. You gotta learn to control your leg if you want to be the strong, silent type. Or just man up and out with it."

"Elsa didn't get the models booked for the show." The words came out before I could stop them.

"Say that again?"

"She thought she had everything in place. Please don't be mad at her."

My grandmother leaned back and closed her eyes. "Oh, Elsa," she whispered. "You can be so endearing and so infuriating." Her eyes opened and looked at me. "I wish your grandfather was here. I relied on his patience to keep me calm at times like this."

"Is the show really ruined?"

She took a big swig of her lemonade.

"Short of a miracle."

# 30

At dinner that night, my father went on and on about ideas he'd been dreaming up for next year's parade float.

"I know this is going to sound crazy, but I was thinking about a circus theme with acrobats and everything."

My mother gave him her everything-you-come-up-with-sounds-crazy look.

"Where are you going to get acrobats? Are you planning to kidnap them the next time a real circus happens through town? As I recall, the last circus that rolled through was shortly before the First World War."

"We don't need professional acrobats. Harley and the boys can do it. They'll steal the show."

Trying to imagine my father's friend Joe swinging through the air on a flying trapeze sent a shiver through me. It would take a trapeze made of military-grade steel to keep him aloft.

"Couldn't you just use the float from this year's parade?" my mother asked.

My father waved his chicken leg in front of him as if warding off evil.

"Molly, we can't just recycle the same marketing year after year. We've got to stay ahead of our fan base's expectations. Keep the element of surprise."

"You have a fan base?"

He took a bite off the leg. "You know what I mean."

I'm pretty sure what he meant was that I should be preparing myself for another round of parade embarrassment next year involving me in a clown costume, or worse yet, acrobat tights.

After dinner, I hung out in the living room playing my favorite levels of *Death Intruders 3*. Somewhere between level eighteen, where the undead visit high school prom, and level twenty-one, where they sneak into the mayor's mansion, I had a sudden idea strike me like a rotted hand. What if local women were the models for the show? If my father thought he could use amateur acrobats for his float, why couldn't we use amateur models for the fashion show? The solution seemed too easy. Honestly, all they had to do was walk up and down the runway a few times.

How hard could that be?

I found Elsa the next morning slumped behind the counter. She looked like she hadn't slept.

"Hi," I said.

"Hi," she squeaked in response.

That led to a long, awkward silence in which I kept waiting for her to say something and she kept staring blankly into space.

"I had an idea that maybe could save the show," I tried.

The word *show* snapped Elsa out of her trance long enough to get off the stool and begin randomly straightening up around the store.

"The show isn't going to happen," she said with calm finality.

"But what if we used local talent for the show?" I continued. "You know, amateurs."

Elsa wandered from display table to display table refolding clothes that didn't need refolding while avoiding facing me.

"It's too late," she said, her voice drifting from someplace far away. "I've canceled everything and got the deposits back already."

I'd never seen Elsa so calm. It was creepy like something out of a horror movie right before a knife appears and blood spurts onto the screen. "But couldn't the reservations be made again?"

She stopped. "I broke up with Harley last night," she answered in a voice even quieter than before. "I'm going to school in the fall, and one day I'm going to own this store and nothing is going to get in the way of that."

Whoa, I knew she was taking things hard. But I had no idea how hard. "Oh."

The rest of the morning stayed pretty much as awkward as it started. Elsa floated about the store like a forlorn ghost haunting the display tables while I hid out in the back room trying desperately to speed the clock up with my mind. After what felt like a haunted house eternity, the clock finally struck two, and I slipped out the front door and away from the ghostly spirit still roaming the aisles.

The fresh air felt good after hours of stuffy uncomfortableness. But the sad look on Elsa's face lingered in my mind. It seemed so unfair that one little mistake could cause such an unholy mess for Elsa and my grandmother, not to mention all the women looking forward to the show—and even Harley, who had been cast as the silent villain for no good reason.

The smell of eggs and bacon drew my attention to the Sunshine Café I happened to be passing. Alone at a table in the corner, Diane sat sipping coffee. At sight of me, she waved. Any other time I would have continued on without even thinking about stopping in to talk to her. But today was different. Maybe because my own life was in ruins, I felt the need to make one last effort on Elsa's behalf. Or maybe it was the smell of bacon.

Diane waved me to an open seat across from her.

"Stu! I'm so glad to see you. How is Elsa holding up?"

Fine, if an eternity spent haunting a clothing store was considered holding up. "Not so good. She's still pretty upset. She broke up with Harley last night."

Diane's coffee mug rattled onto the table.

"The girl did what last night?"

"She broke up with Harley," I repeated.

"Why on earth did she do that?"

"She acted like she had to make a choice between Harley and the store. And she chose the store."

Diane shook her head.

"It's so hard being a woman these days. I get where she's coming from. But that girl needs some help understanding she doesn't have to choose between her career and her man. Unless the man is trying to force her to quit her career. In which case, the man has to go. But I didn't get the impression Harley was like that."

The whole discussion was whistling past over my head. Why would a woman feel like they had to make a choice? "It seemed like he wanted to help her make the show a success," I threw out. "They seemed like a good team together."

"I agree. There must be something we can do to help keep this whole thing from blowing up sky high."

Diane had a practical common sense that renewed a tiny bit of hope. Maybe there was still a chance for my idea. "I thought of something last night," I began. "What if we did the show using local talent? You know, amateur models instead of hiring professionals. Couldn't that work?"

"Amateurs? You mean like ladies in town?"

Time to name names and put it all on the line. "Yeah, like maybe you, and Mildred, and Audrey, and Aiko, and maybe some others."

A laugh bubbled up from deep inside Diane's chest.

"Well, that's an interesting idea. But might be a bit harder to convince the models than you're thinking. Watching a fashion show is one thing, but strutting on the catwalk being gawked at is another."

She slid her last piece of bacon onto a napkin and pushed it over to me.

"With that said, you just might have the answer that saves the show. Let me chat with your grandmother and see what I can do."

Free bacon and Diane's help. What more could I want?

**32**

I strolled back out into the sunshine. Sometimes when life throws you a curve, you just have to adjust your swing and smack that baby out of the ballpark. I wasn't a hero. Just an ordinary guy taking action in a heroic sort of way. If it led to a movie deal and an action figure, so be it.

Ahead, a couple crossed the street with their two little girls heading for the ice cream shop. Something seemed familiar about that family, as if I'd seen them before. The hero in me dropped to its knees. Every superhero has their kryptonite, mine came with a lone chin hair. Seeing Jackson and Becca together again liquefied my self-esteem into a cape-less puddle of envy in the middle of the sidewalk.

As I watched, Jackson held the door open for the

girls to enter. He gave Becca a playful push as the door closed, locking them in and me out. The crazy thought passed through my head that maybe I should join them. In a matter of moments, I could be enjoying a tasty frozen treat while in the company of friends. I'm sure they wouldn't mind. Would they? Or would it be the most awkward moment in the history of all awkward moments?

While my brain remained frozen with indecision, my feet took action and hurried me the opposite direction in a fit of speed walking that would have made Olympic speed walkers jealous. I couldn't get away fast enough from the possibility of Becca and Jackson sharing a double scoop of rocky road. I suddenly found myself inside the hardware store owned by Ben's father, holding a package of Hot Wheels cars for comfort. If only I could be ten again and spend my summer safe in the toy aisle.

"What's happenin'?"

Ben gave me his typical annoying grin.

"Nothing."

He took the package of cars and eyed them closely.

"I see you found the new Flower Patch cars."

I grabbed the package back and looked more closely. The cars inside were shaped like garden bugs and painted to match. The ladybug car was especially cute, if only I was three and into flowers and cute little bugs. The package went back on the shelf.

"Shut up."

Ben put a hand on my forehead.

"Dude, you must be burning up. What sort of fever does it take to get into Flower Patch cars?"

"A fever as big as your head."

"That doesn't even make sense."

He had a point. But it was the best I could do given that globs of rocky road ice cream were dancing in the periphery of my vision.

"I need to play *Death Intruders*." Anything to get my mind off that ice cream shop.

"Sure. I get off at four. Come to my house then."

By 4:00 p.m., I was a nervous wreck. Not only had I been unsuccessful in keeping my mind occupied while waiting, but I had to pass Becca's house to get to Ben's. Ducking low behind a line of cars on the far side of the street, I ran past like a soldier skirting an enemy outpost.

After being chased by ravenously hungry zombies for a couple hours, I finally calmed down enough to help Ben polish off a bag of Cheetos.

"I can't believe your mom buys Cheetos."

"They complement the cases of orange soda in the pantry."

He had a point. Their pantry looked like an autumn sunset, all orangey on the lower shelves with hints of yellow at the top.

"Don't eat the corn chips," Ben said, taking the unopened bag in my hands and putting it back on the top shelf. "My mom is saving those for a party they're hosting this weekend."

"I should get home," I said. "My dad's making burgers again. He takes it personally if I don't have at least two."

Ben showed me to the door. "I'm with ya. A guy's gotta do what a guy's gotta do."

As I neared the corner, my eyes drifted up the cascade of flowers spilling down the rock-retaining wall leading up to Becca's house. At the top, the porch swing swayed slowly in the breeze. Except there was no breeze, only Becca swaying back and forth, her bare feet lightly pushing off with each swing. The zombie warlord in my chest let out a strangled scream before clawing through my intestines in a failed attempt to hide behind my colon from the terror lurking above.

Becca locked eyes with me but didn't smile or wave. Instead, she seemed unsure how to respond to my sudden appearance. I was pretty sure if I held up a mirror I would find the exact same expression plastered on my own face. For the second time that day, I froze in indecision. Should I wave? Say hello? Or wait for her to make the first move? After all, I wasn't the one hanging out with Jackson every day.

Before I could decide, she got up and went inside. And that's when the ugly reality hit me: things with Becca were messed up for real.

The next few days dragged by in a low-hanging haze of awkwardness. At the store, an uncomfortable silence replaced the chatty gleefulness that had always been Elsa. I missed the old Elsa and her enthusiasm about the simplest things like what color crepe paper to order for the gift boxes or how to make the model in the display window seem cheerier.

All her moping also pretty much ruined any chance of her helping me with the nightmare my love life had become. *Love life* seemed a bit of an exaggeration. But the knot in the pit of my stomach felt otherwise. Every time I thought of Becca and Jackson together it felt like zombies were feasting on my internal organs. I shuddered to think what an X-ray of my abdomen would look like. Probably a pile of bloody pulp with a few rotted teeth still clinging to the remains of my liver.

"Is the show still on?"

The same question came up every time a customer entered the store. Each time the haunted shopkeeper known as Elsa would fidget from one foot to the other.

"It's been canceled this year," she'd explain in a high quavering voice that sounded from beyond the grave. "Due to circumstances beyond our control."

"Oh, that's a shame," the person would reply.

I would nod in agreement like the mournful cemetery keeper I had become. After days listening to Elsa's voice, my nerves were frayed.

"Is the show still on?" a lovely little lady in her seventies asked, staring innocently up at Elsa.

"No," I interrupted before having to listen to Elsa moan for the umpteenth time. "It's not!"

The shocked look on the woman's face complemented the glare Elsa gave me.

"What was that all about?" Elsa asked after the little lady shuffled out without looking back.

"I don't know. Why don't we just put up a big sign that says, *No show this year. Stop asking.*"

Elsa went to work refolding blouses on a display table.

"It's my fault. The least I can do is face our customers straight up. I'm not going to hide behind a sign."

"Well, that sucks."

"What sucks?"

"You moping around the store every day. And everybody who comes in always being all disappointed. And this summer being pretty much the worst summer ever."

Elsa paused.

"I didn't realize the show meant that much to you. Is there something else going on?"

I should have kept my mouth shut. "No."

She peered at me closer.

"Just avoiding your problems doesn't make them go away."

"Isn't that what *you're* doing?"

She idly twisted the collar of the blouse she was holding slowly strangling it.

"I just said I'm *facing* the customers, not *avoiding* them."

"Really?" my voice rose to match hers. "Aren't you hiding here every day when the show could still happen if you gave it a chance?"

Elsa twisted the collar of the defenseless blouse further.

"There's NO possible way to save the show, and you know it!" she shouted. "Who are you to tell me about giving up? You're the one who won't talk to your own girlfriend."

"And you're the one who broke up with Harley for no reason!" The words came out before I could stop them.

The blouse dangled lifeless in her hands.

"HOW DARE YOU CRITICIZE ME! I AM NOT A BAD PERSON!"

"Well," Diane said, barging through the front door. "Looks like I'm arriving just in the nick of time."

She marched over, took the blouse from Elsa, and smoothed out the wrinkles.

"The two of you have been under a lot of stress. But things are about to take a turn for the better, just you believe me."

She set down the blouse and took Elsa under one

wing. Elsa covered her mouth with one hand.

"I'm—I'm so sorry," she gasped. "I—I haven't been sleeping—and—and I just lost it."

Tears streaked down her cheeks. I checked my own to make sure I wasn't copying her. The corners of my eyes felt like tiny fire hoses ready to douse my burning cheeks, but I wasn't about to let that happen in public. "I'm all right," I said, even though no one had asked the question.

Diane motioned me over and swept me beneath her other wing.

"You are two of the most amazing young people I have ever known. Everything is going to be okay."

She released us and headed for the front door.

"C'mon, we've got a little adventure ahead of us."

Elsa gave me an is-she-out-of-her-mind? look.

"What? But we can't leave the store unattended."

Diane waved for us to follow.

"Just this one time it will be okay. Your grand-mother's waiting in my car. Lock up and let's go."

"I think it's okay," I said. "Just this one time."

Elsa considered for a moment before finally flipping the OPEN sign to CLOSED and locking the front door.

"Okay," she said. "I'm trusting you."

Great. I knew how that usually ended.

**34**

Elsa and I sat in the back as Diane drove out of town into the countryside.

"Where are we going?" Elsa asked.

"You'll see," my grandmother replied.

After a couple miles and a few more turns, we eased down a long gravel drive that brought us to a big red barn situated behind a picture-perfect farmhouse. In the old days, there had been a lot of dairy farms in Sequim. My dad says there used to be cows roaming everywhere. But that was a long time ago. All that's left now are old cross rail fences trimmed with barbed wire, and a few dilapidated barns slowly slumping over.

"Here we are!" Diane announced as we climbed out of her car.

An elderly man climbed out of a fancy black BMW

parked nearby. He wore a navy-blue sport coat and matching navy-blue slacks with brown dress shoes so polished they gleamed in the sunlight. He greeted my grandmother with a kiss on both cheeks.

"My dear," he said. "So good to see you again so soon."

"I think you know Stefan," my grandmother said to Elsa. "He owns Town and Country, the men's fashion store in Port Angeles."

He kissed both of Elsa's cheeks.

"Elsa, Rosemarie's beautiful protégé."

Her cheeks flushed. "Yes, we've met."

A woman exited the house and approached.

"Diane, lovely to see you!"

She took us all in.

"And I see you've brought everyone with you. Shall I show you around?"

"That would be lovely," Diane replied.

The woman led the way into the barn. From the outside, it looked pretty much like any other big old red barn. But inside was a different matter. Everyone gasped.

"It's a beauty, isn't it?" Diane asked.

Wood beams soared overhead like some sort of medieval church. All the windows had been replaced with stained glass and the woodwork restored and oiled. Wagon-wheel chandeliers hung from the rafters and sconces with gaslights glowed warm orange along the walls. Fresh wood chips covered the floor and filled the room with a pine scent. There wasn't a sign of hay bales, farm animals, or cow poop anywhere.

"What is this place?" I asked.

The woman giving the tour smiled.

"We call it the Farm Cathedral. Took two years and most of our life savings to restore. We book it mostly for weddings. People come from all over to be married here. The cathedral can seat three hundred guests, and with the barn doors open, there's standing room for at least a hundred more."

"And it's available?" my grandmother asked.

The woman patted my grandmother on the arm.

"We had a late cancellation. I'm afraid not every wedding happens as planned. In this case, they gave notice too late for a refund. Lucky that Diane called me when she did! We'd be proud to host your show."

"Wait a minute," Elsa interrupted. "What's going on here?"

"My dear," my grandmother said, turning to Elsa. "The show needs to happen."

"It's too late for that," Elsa countered.

"Honey," Diane said. "It ain't never too late for redemption."

My grandmother moved directly in front of Elsa and waited until their eyes met.

"The thing is people are counting on it. And you and I are not the sort of folks to let our disappointment get in the way of our duty to our customers. So, this is going to be the year you get your wish. We're going to make this the biggest, grandest fashion show we've ever hosted."

The look on Elsa's face changed from vacant stare to wide-eyed disbelief.

"You want to do the show with Stefan?"

"Yep. If my hip has taught me anything, it's that change is part of life. I know in the past I haven't been keen on the idea. But the store is going to be yours one day. It's time I started opening myself to new ideas. Your ideas!"

"But what about the models?"

My grandmother turned to me.

"We've got a new partner in this operation, and I think we should listen to what he has to say."

"You mean you're okay using amateurs?" Elsa asked.

"Not only am I okay with it," my grandmother answered, "I think it's a grand idea that will make the show unlike anything our customers have ever seen."

"I don't know. An awful lot needs to happen in two weeks. Do you think we can really pull it off?"

Diane put an arm around Elsa's shoulders.

"Just look around you, honey. In this place, anything is possible."

Elsa nodded.

"Okay, if everyone's on board. I'll call the rental company and caterer right away."

The next few days flew by in a flurry of activity at the store. Elsa and Stefan met for hours selecting the outfits for the show. My father brought my grandmother's sewing machine and set it up in one corner. And the new models stopped in continually to be fitted.

"The new models aren't quite the size of the models we were expecting," my grandmother explained. "And when I say not quite the same size I mean it might be quicker to sew new outfits from scratch."

She held up a suit coat the size of a dump truck.

"Your father's friend Joe is one mountain of a man."

That was for darn sure. For the record, I'm not the one responsible for the meat float crew being asked to model. My father proposed them and against all better judgment my grandmother agreed that it was a splendid idea. Clearly, she had missed the parade.

"But he's also the kindest man I've ever met," she continued. "He brought me flowers as a thank-you when *he's* the one helping *me* out. Wouldn't it be nice if everyone were that kind?"

His bat striking the papier-mâché bunny on the meat float popped to mind. "Uh, yeah."

Dozens of people visited the store daily to check out the clothing for the show or to ask questions about the event. And not just women, either. Word had spread that men were being included this year. At times, there were more men than women in the store.

"Finally, men are being treated equally," an elderly man with a silver beard said, checking out the suits hanging next to my grandmother as she worked.

"Oh, yes," my grandmother quipped back. "Equal rights for men have been a real concern for years. If only you could be given more advantages in life."

The man gave me a wink.

"She's got a point there, you know. We've been on

top for a very long time. But women are the future. You mark my words. Their turn has come, and it's way overdue."

That brought a smile to my grandmother's face.

"All right, you can stand there and appreciate my work."

"This material is divine," Diane commented as my grandmother marked the hem of her corduroy skirt."

My grandmother made one last chalk mark, then stepped back.

"Diane, you're all good to go. Just leave the skirt on the pile next to my sewing machine after you change out of it."

Diane remained in place, her hands fidgeting with the corduroy folds of the skirt.

"Everything okay?" my grandmother asked.

A flush crept up Diane's face as she stared at herself in the mirror next to the sewing machine.

"Are you sure you want people like . . . me going up onstage? I'm not exactly the shape of your everyday model."

Aiko stepped close and took Diane's hand.

"You are beautiful in every way."

Diane blushed and dabbed at an eye.

"Thank you, Aiko. I'm sorry to be all self-conscious, but I've never been asked to model in a show. Or anywhere else. I just don't want to disappoint anyone."

My grandmother put down the chalk and took Diane's other hand.

"My dear, there is no one, and I mean no one, I would rather have on that runway. You are going to be a sensation!"

The three women hugged. It had never occurred to me until that moment that Diane, the sky-blue shopping ringleader who always seemed so sure of herself, could have insecurities. Could it be that everyone, even adults, had moments when they felt unsure? The idea seemed crazy, and yet only days ago I had watched Elsa whimper like a middle schooler. It was enough to make me wonder if anyone ever really grew up.

Near the end of the week, my grandmother pulled me aside.

"Stu, I could really use you and a few of your friends to be in the show. Elsa and Stefan want to include some younger fashions to encourage younger customers to visit our stores. It would help me out if you stepped up."

There's nothing worse than being needed by your grandmother, especially when her need forces you to confront problems you're desperately trying to avoid.

"I'll talk to them."

"When?"

"Soon."

"How soon?"

Geez, you'd think the show was only a week away.

"The show is only a week away," she said as if reading my thoughts. "I'll give you the weekend, but I need to know by Monday morning. Okay?"

That gave me two days to figure things out with Becca. Or think of a better plan. I could only hope I'd come up with something better.

**36**

I spent the evening contemplating my options. Join a passing circus got ruled out early. It was a great plan but required a passing circus. Finding a passing circus required a method of time travel back to the days when passing circuses existed. And that required a mad scientist with a time machine I could borrow. To be honest, I couldn't even find my new electric toothbrush let alone a mad scientist with a spare time machine.

Option two required asking someone other than Becca to be my partner for the show. Gretchen popped to mind. A fit of gagging left me gasping for breath. So much for option two. That left me with option three.

There was no option three. Really, there was no

option one or two, either. My only option was to let my grandmother down gently and accept the consequences. Goodbye, cash-filled envelopes for Christmas.

"Stu, there's someone at the door asking for you."

That seemed odd. My mother never announced when one of my friends came over. They usually just tackled me unawares from behind.

"It's a girl," she added.

A girl? The zombie warlord woke. I could only think of one girl who had ever set foot on our doorstep. Had she been in the neighborhood and simply stopped by to say hi? Or had she finally worked up the nerve to break the news that she and Jackson were eloping to Canada? The first idea seemed a bit too coincidental. And the second a tad bit paranoid, which made it all the more likely.

I dragged myself downstairs only to stop short at sight of Kirsten standing on our porch. She motioned with one finger for me to step outside.

"I brought you this," she said, holding out an envelope.

I took it and stared at my name written in neat cursive on the front.

"It's an invitation," she continued, "to Becca's birthday party."

I opened the envelope and pulled out the card inside. *Please join me to celebrate my 13th birthday at Sequim Bay State Park* was written in fancy lettering. Crayon-colored balloons floated along the edges above hand-drawn evergreen trees. The invitation closed with *Can't wait! Becca.* It all looked just the way we'd planned it that day at Lake Crescent.

"Why are you being such a jerk?"

Kirsten's words struck me like a punch in the gut. What was she talking about? What had I done? "What—?"

"You know, the way you keep treating her."

"But—"

"All you do is ignore her."

"But—"

"You walk past her house without even saying hi. What's wrong with you?"

What's wrong with me? Weren't we leaving out the

obvious? She didn't even like me anymore. She was too busy with her new boyfriend, Jackson, to care about me. "But she and—"

Maybe it was the terror in my eyes, but Kirsten's angry stare softened.

"You really don't know anything, do you?" she said slowly, as if speaking to a dim-witted guy who knew nothing about girls.

Now we were getting somewhere.

"But—I thought—"

She shook her head and turned to go.

"She's not going to wait around forever for you to figure out what you want."

I stood on the porch watching her march off down the street. Had Becca sent Kirsten to give me that message? Or was it simply Kirsten being Kirsten and sticking her nose in where it didn't belong? If I believed her, then maybe it wasn't too late. But if she was wrong, I would look like a total idiot if I asked Becca to be my partner for the show and she said no. What was I supposed to do?

By dinnertime, I had reached a simple conclusion: I

would never understand girls and probably die a lonely bachelor after a lifetime wandering the earth wondering how everything always ended up being my fault.

"I hear the fashion show is back on," my father said between mouthfuls of spaghetti. "And it's going to be bigger than ever."

I kept my eyes down, pretending the statement had been meant for someone else.

"Stu, is it true that the show is going to also have men's fashions this year?" my mother prompted.

Honestly, what difference did it make? While I had wasted my summer working at my grandmother's store some clod with a lone chin hair had wooed my almost girlfriend away.

"Maybe," I answered.

"Maybe?" my father asked. "Don't you know?"

Of course I knew. "Yes! The show is with Stefan this year. So what?"

My mother tipped her head to one side.

"Is there something going on?" she asked.

"No, everything's fine."

My father slurped a line of spaghetti into his mouth.

"Is it about working at your grandmother's store?"

It was about everything. But that stupid store didn't help. "How long do I have to keep working there? I look like an idiot hanging out with dresses, and pantsuits, and stuff!"

My father leaned back and assessed my spindly arms, and birdlike beak of a face.

"I guess you've got a point there. Maybe it would be reasonable to see if your grandmother can find someone else to help out after the show."

I stabbed a meatball and jammed it into my mouth. "I don't need someone else to take over for me. I'm fine!"

My father gave my mother a helpless look.

"Your father was just trying to help," my mother said.

Really? The sort of help I needed involved a traveling circus and a time machine.

"I'm fine," I said again.

"Fine," my brother repeated, rolling a meatball like a

steamroller over his noodles.

"Your moods are a little hard to predict these days," my mother said.

"It's like living with an ever-changing weather system," my father added. "It's hard to keep up. And your sun breaks seem to be getting fewer and farther between."

Since when did dinner become a weather report? And what did they know about anything? They sat around every day being all happily married and not having to worry about anything important. My life wasn't anything like theirs. And they couldn't possibly understand. It wasn't like they had ever been kids. I set my fork down and pushed away from the table. "I'm done."

The look on my mother's face shifted from mostly exasperated to more than a little worried.

"Are you sure? You don't want dessert? There's ice cream."

The mention of ice cream brought back the memory of Becca and Jackson at the ice cream shop together. I'd never be able to eat ice cream again. "Maybe later."

Out on the front porch, I slumped down on the steps. Chester, our Labrador retriever, plunked down next to me and gave me the goofy grin he always gave no matter how the world treated him, or how horrible it treated anyone else. Being a dog was the ideal life. Eat, sleep, and repeat. My hand scratched the fur behind his ear. He leaned until his head pressed against me. If only we could trade places, he could be the one fidgeting in his own skin and I could be the one moaning from the simple pleasure of having my ear scratched.

Deep down, I knew exactly what I need to do. March over to Becca's house and have the conversation I'd been needing to have with her for weeks. Did she like me? Were we going out? Or had I been living in the undead reality of my own fantasy world in which a scrawny kid of average size and intelligence could actually be going out with someone like her? The truth seemed all too obvious. And yet I needed to know. Soon.

# 37

The slow walk to Becca's house reminded me of the slow walk I took in the spring when I had visited to apologize after bleeding all over the back of her head. Those days seemed like an eternity ago. It wasn't my nose that felt broken this time. That break healed in a few weeks. This one would probably take a lifetime.

Just as I turned onto her street, my father roared up in his truck and swerved onto the sidewalk next to me.

"C'mon, get in!" he shouted.

The shock of his sudden appearance froze my feet in place. "What?"

His arm reached through the open window and slapped the side of the truck.

"I said c'mon, get in!" he shouted again. "We gotta go!"

My father never slapped anything, let alone his beloved truck. The sound of his hand striking the metal snapped me to attention. "What's wrong?"

He waved at the passenger door.

"I'll explain on the way. Just get in!"

We spun around and swerved onto the next street before speeding through town without even slowing for traffic lights.

"Is it Grandma?" I shouted over the roar of the engine.

In the distance, a line of smoke rose into the evening sky.

"No, your grandmother is fine. But I'm afraid the show is in jeopardy."

We swerved onto another road, the same road Diane had used when taking us to visit the Farm Cathedral. The line of smoke grew into a black column up ahead.

"Is that the barn?"

The truck slid sideways as we turned down the long gravel driveway. Two fire engines blocked the parking area. Beyond the fire engines, the barn looked like some sort of fire-breathing monster with flames spurting out a hole in the roof.

"C'mon," my father said, waving me after him as he ran from the truck.

A small crowd of people had gathered to watch as the firefighters fought the blaze with fire hoses from two sides in an attempt to quench the monster's thirst. My nose twitched from the smell of burning wood and wafting smoke stung my eyes. On the house's porch, the woman who had given us the tour hid her head against a man's chest.

"What happened?" my father asked the guy standing next to us.

He shook his head.

"Don't know for sure. My guess is an electrical fire. Started about half an hour ago."

He pointed to a house in the distance.

"Lived there forty years. Never seen anything like this."

My father nodded.

"One of my buddies is a volunteer firefighter. He called me on his way here."

He turned to me.

"Your mother is calling your grandmother right now. It's a bummer about the show. But even more of a bummer for the Wilsons. They put everything into fixing this place up. What a shame for them."

A third fire engine rumbled down the drive. A police officer moved the crowd out of the way for it to park next to the other two. I could see Mrs. Wilson and her husband still standing on the porch leaning on each other. My problems suddenly didn't seem quite so important. I couldn't imagine what it must feel like to have years of work go up in smoke in a matter of minutes.

"Will they be all right?"

My father put a hand on my shoulder.

"They're good people. It'll take time for them to recover. Sometimes all you can do is pick up the pieces and start over again. It won't be easy. But, yeah, they'll be all right."

The third firefighting crew joined the first two. Together they battled the fire from three sides. Water poured over the barn roof like a torrential downpour. At last, the flames stopped spewing and the smoke changed from a thick black column to a hazy shroud covering the barn in a smoky fog.

My father put his arm around me, and we headed back up the driveway.

"I think we've seen enough," he said.

Things can turn so quickly. It was hard to believe that such a beautiful place could burn in a matter of minutes. "Everything had finally gotten worked out for the show," I said. "Now it's all ruined."

We climbed back into my father's truck.

"Don't be so sure," my father said. "Sometimes a silver lining is just around the corner waiting to be found."

Yeah, right.

I arrived at work the next morning to find Stefan, Elsa, Diane, and my grandmother circled around my grandmother's sewing machine deep in discussion.

"—and we can't possibly find a venue that will work with so little time left," Stefan continued. "Our joint endeavor must end here."

"But we've come too far to give up now," Diane countered. "There has to be a way."

My grandmother lifted her cane.

"My friends, the fashion gods have turned against us this year. We've all made a valiant effort, but I'm forced to agree with Stefan. The show simply cannot go on."

"It's all my fault," Elsa said quietly. "If I hadn't messed everything up—"

"My dear," my grandmother interrupted. "You can hardly fault yourself for an electrical fire."

Elsa's shoulders slumped. "I guess so. But if I had reserved the models like I was supposed to, then we would have had the show here and none of this would have happened."

Stefan held up a finger.

"Elsa makes a great point. If I withdraw from the show, the show can still take place here as originally planned. That is the only reasonable solution. You must go on without me."

"No!" my grandmother said with authority. "We've come too far to toss you out now. Either this show happens in all its glory or not at all. And that decision is not up for discussion."

Elsa nodded in agreement.

"Why not do the show here anyway?" Diane asked. "Not everyone will get in. And believe me there will be some disappointed folks. But at least the show can still happen."

"We can't fit more than a hundred people at best," my grandmother explained. "We've already had over two hundred and fifty people RSVP to attend. I can't tell them they're uninvited. I'd rather cancel the show than do that to them."

"Well, then I for one am getting out of town," Diane said, dabbing one eye. "I can't be here the day of the show and pretend everything's okay."

Stefan forced a grin. "Yes, perhaps that is what we should all do. Ride off into the sunset on Harleys the day of the show."

My grandmother pursed her lips. "The idea does have a certain if-I-were-young appeal. But there's not a Harley on earth that can take the sting from what I'm feeling right now."

Not a Harley on earth? An idea gnawed its way into my consciousness. Could the solution be that simple? Not that there was anything simple about the solution that had come to mind. If anything, it'd be easier to steal a Harley and ride off with my grandmother and Stefan into the sunset than face the task that I suddenly knew needed to be done.

"Excuse me," I mumbled. "I need to go run an errand."

"Perhaps you can bring us all back some ice cream," my grandmother suggested, trying to force a smile. "We could use a break about now."

Agreed. But the sort of break I had in mind was too big to fit into a cup or cone.

There's a reason I walk rather than ride my bike places. I remembered this the moment I pulled my piece-of-crud bike out of the garage. My parents salvaged it from the thrift store when I was nine. Somewhere in the long-ago past, it had probably been a kid's prized possession with its banana seat, curving handlebars, and sparkly purple fenders.

However, time had not been kind. Currently, white fluff poked from tears in the seat, the fenders were covered in rust, and the chain rattled even when not being peddled. Worst of all, it was perfectly sized for a nine-year-old kid but terribly sized for a guy teetering on the edge of puberty. But what was I supposed to do? Walk all the way to Harley's?

Halfway there, I concluded I should've walked after the air in the back tire spewed out and the rubber started peeling off the rim. I pulled to the side of the road and evaluated my options. Either the bike had to be left in the ditch or I did. The bike had a better chance of success with Harley, but the ditch smelled funny and the trickle of water at the bottom looked like it had oozed from an open sore. I could only hope the bike had the good sense to climb out and hitch a ride with a kindly family before I returned to claim it.

Bike-less, the last mile breezed past like a middle school death march with only the occasional cow mooing to mark my progress. What exactly was I doing out here anyway? Since when did the fashion show matter enough for me to be trekking cross-country on its behalf?

I rounded the last corner and halted in Harley's driveway. The time for truth had arrived. I felt sure he wouldn't throw me off his property but whether he'd hang me from Barb's barbwire armpit was another matter. The sound of hammering drew me to Harley's workshop in the barn. I found him bent over an anvil with a hammer in one hand and a red-hot metal fence post in the other.

"Hey, Harley," I called out.

The hammering stopped. He pulled his safety glasses up.

"Stu! What brings you here?"

Yeah, about that. "Umm . . . just thought I'd stop by and see what you're up to."

He wiped the sweat off his forehead with one arm.

"Is your dad with you?"

"No, just me. I was in the neighborhood."

He gave me a questioning look that seemed entirely appropriate since he lived in the middle of cow fields and his only neighbors were the mooing kind. I had just met several of them on my walk.

"I'm sorry, *what* brings you here?"

What brings me here? Well, the bike for darn sure hadn't. Really, neither had my feet. Something deeper had drawn me. Something I couldn't quite explain but that gnawed at the edges of my mind. Or maybe I was just gullible. Probably just gullible.

"Well—I wanted to—you know—uh—talk to you—like about something."

If that didn't clarify things I didn't know what would. At least I had spoken real words.

Harley scratched his chin. His eyebrows furrowed.

"I'm not quite sure I'm following you."

Geez, did I have to spell it out?

"Well, my grandmother invited Stefan to do the show with her this year, using local models."

"Yeah, I heard that."

"It was going to be at this big, really cool barn outside town. But it had a fire last night."

"The Wilsons' barn?"

"Yeah, and now the show is ruined unless we can find another place where we can have the show. A place big enough for everyone."

That was the easy part. Now for the part that might lead to me being hung from a barbed wire armpit.

"And I was wondering . . . if maybe . . . we could use your barn for the show?"

Harley took a step back. His hammer dropped onto the workbench behind him.

"Did Elsa put you up to this?"

"No, she doesn't know," I said in a rush. "She's still really upset about—well, everything that's happened."

He sagged against the workbench. For a moment, he looked exactly how I felt the last time I saw Becca turning away on her porch and closing the door behind her.

"She hurt me pretty bad," he said.

My conversation with Elsa came back to mind.

"She seems afraid she'll have to give up her career."

He stuck the red-hot fence post into a bucket of water. Steam hissed in a cloud around him.

"That's crazy. I like that she has a life of her own. Something that she's passionate about. I would never ask her to give that up. Not in a million years."

"Maybe you just need to show her that."

He rubbed his face with both hands.

"I don't know. I kinda wear my emotions on my sleeve. I don't know if I'm willing to risk it again."

"Oh."

He slumped further, a giant of a man reduced to the size of a frightened middle school kid.

"I don't know," he repeated to himself.

He stood that way for what seemed like forever. Until his hands clenched. And his knees straightened. And his shoulders lifted as if he was slowly being filled back up with air. Suddenly, he stood before me like the giant-of-a-man Harley I had always known.

"But the thing is, she's worth it," he said. "She's worth it and I can't forever mope around heartbroken like I've been doing most my life. And even if she doesn't want me back, it's the right thing to do for her, and for your grandmother."

The fire in his eyes burned hotter than the glow of the metal fencepost he had been holding. Okay, I might be exaggerating a bit. But something was going on in that man, and I, for one, was happy to once again be looking up at my larger-than-life superhero Harley.

"I got a lot of work to do," he said. "If you'll excuse me, I'm gonna get going. A few days isn't much time to make this place fashion-show ready."

That was for darn sure.

**40**

I found Diane and my grandmother huddled together at a corner table in the Sunshine Café.

"You look like you've been walking for hours," Diane observed.

If dragging a broken-down bike for miles counts as walking. "Pretty much."

"What have you been up to?" my grandmother asked, passing me the other half of her turkey sandwich.

I wolfed down the sandwich along with the glass of Coke the waitress set in front of me.

"I found a venue for the show."

"You what?!" Diane exclaimed.

"Yeah," I continued. "Harley was hesitant at first, but he seems really excited about having the show in his barn."

My grandmother choked on her iced tea.

"What did you just say?"

"Uh . . . I said Harley was kinda hesitant at first but then he thought about it and agreed to host the show in his barn."

My grandmother pushed her iced tea away as if it had just been poisoned.

"Are we talking about the same Harley?" she asked. "And the same barn?"

"Maybe he has a new barn," Diane added, patting my grandmother's hand.

She and my grandmother exchanged looks. Not good looks. Frightened looks like two rabbits about to cross a busy highway.

"Any other ideas?" my grandmother whispered.

"Not one," Diane replied.

My grandmother massaged her hip and let out a heavy sigh.

"Stefan might agree if we don't let him see the barn. But Elsa. I don't know how she'll respond."

She asked the server for the check, then stood.

"Guess there's only one way to find out."

We traipsed into the store and found Elsa behind the counter with shoulders slumped.

"My dear," my grandmother said. "Take a moment from what you're doing. We'd like to discuss something with you."

Elsa looked up. The vacant ghostly stare had returned.

"What is it?" she asked in her mournful voice.

"The three of us have been talking," my grandmother continued. "And we've come up with a rather ingenious solution to save the show."

"Harley's barn," I squeaked.

The look on Elsa's face switched from haunted to terrified.

"What? We can't," she faltered. "Not after what I did to him. I can't face him again."

As if on cue, the door opened, and Harley entered. He stood in the entry like an Old West gunslinger brandishing a black vest and boots, his greasy handle-bar mustache glimmering in the neon light.

"Oh my," Diane whispered, fanning herself.

"Am I interrupting?" Harley asked.

Elsa went rigid. "What is he doing here?" she whispered.

Diane gave her a friendly push forward.

"Talk to the boy. I think you owe him that."

Elsa shuffled to where Harley stood waiting.

"They just told me you offered the use of your barn for the show."

Harley hesitated, avoiding her eyes.

"Stu came by earlier. He said you needed a bigger place for the show. I know my barn's not the most beautiful thing, but it has enough space and I've come up with some plans to make it look nicer for the show."

He pulled a paper from his pocket and handed it to Elsa. She unfolded it and stared at the drawings.

"Can you really do all this?" she asked.

He paused to consider.

"There's not a lot of time to work with, but I think I can get pretty close to what you see there," he replied.

She leaned in closer, her voice lowering.

"This doesn't change things. I just can't be in a serious relationship right now."

Harley nodded, though I could see the hurt in his eyes.

"I think it's great that you have a career you're passionate about," he continued. "I get that. And I want to do something to help you and Rosemarie and the store. If you'll let me."

The faintest smile curved her lips.

"We don't have much time and a lot to do to get ready. I hope you're up for it."

His grin matched hers.

"I better get going. I got a list of things to get at the hardware store. Just wanted to stop by and make sure the show was still on."

He nodded to the rest of us, then exited. Diane shook her head.

"Honey, you got yourself something there that you do *not* want to let go."

"Well," my grandmother agreed. "Looks like the show is back on again."

She gave me a hard stare.

"Including finding the last models for the show, right?"

That woman was relentless.

"Uh—yeah."

The next few minutes seemed almost peaceful after all that had happened in the last few hours. Elsa got on the phone to make arrangements and my grandmother went straight to work on the pile of alterations still waiting to be cut and stitched.

The moment they were both busy, Diane pulled me aside.

"Do you think Harley can really turn that barn into something suitable for a fashion show all by himself in less than a week?"

My memory of the barn came into sharp relief. The dirt floor littered with piles of dried cow dung. The beams and walls covered in cobwebs like a Halloween haunted house. And no lights anywhere except in his workshop. "Sure."

She gave me her you-can't-fool-me look.

"I appreciate your loyalty. He's a wonderful young

man with a heart of gold. But is there anyone who can help him?"

When I thought about it, Harley overhauling his barn alone in a matter of a few days did seem optimistic. "He and my dad and the rest of the meat float crew are pretty tight. I'm sure they'd be willing to lend a hand."

Diane brightened. "That's a great idea. Why don't I stay here and help Elsa while you run over to your dad's shop and ask him?" She leaned in conspiratorially. "We can keep it our little secret for now. No use worrying Elsa and your grandmother. They have enough to worry about already. Sound good?"

Uh, sure.

**41**

A burst of optimism swelled inside as I headed up Sequim Avenue. Yes, the show had been on the brink of ruin, but that didn't mean things couldn't still turn out all right. With my dad's help and the meat float crew backing him up, anything was possible. Looking around I couldn't help but notice the sky shimmering blue and the day bright with opportunity.

Why, right there in front of me a lovely young lady had just stepped out of Ben's father's hardware store. The zombie warlord grabbed my larynx and attempted to strangle me from the inside out.

Becca turned, and our eyes met.

"Uh, h-hi," I stammered.

She hesitated, her lips trembling.

"Hi."

The entirety of the debate over asking her to be my partner for the show flashed through my mind in a jumbled blur of anxiety-riddled confusion. The simple conclusion: there would never be a better chance than the one in front of me right now.

"Hey—um—I was wondering—"

The door behind Becca opened, and her little sister, Carly, exited onto the sidewalk holding a plastic tool belt filled with plastic tools.

"My mom promised her a tool belt if she did all her chores for two straight weeks," Becca explained.

"Oh, that's nice," I mumbled, trying to regain my focus despite the tool-belt-wielding distraction tugging on Becca's arm. "Um—like I was saying—I think you know the fashion show is happening this Saturday right before your party."

"Yes," Becca replied. "My family is planning to come."

"Becca," Carly whined.

Becca pulled her arm out of Carly's grasp. "Just wait a minute," she scolded.

Her eyes turned back to me.

"Um—well—the thing is—I was wondering—"

The door opened again, and Carly's best friend, Jess, exited carrying a tool belt of her own.

"Becca," Carly whined again. "Let's go."

Becca snorted like an angry bull. "Will you be quiet?" she snapped at her sister. "Just be patient for one minute."

She gave me a shrug. "This is what my days are like."

Time was running out. I needed to just up and ask her and get it over with.

"Look, the thing is, my grandmother wants me and a couple of my friends to model in the show. It will mean walking the runway just like the adults. And— anyway—I was wondering if—"

The door opened again, and a creature from the deep suddenly appeared, his lone chin hair gleaming in the sunlight. The zombie warlord staggered back against my rib cage. He was with her? Now?

"Hey, Stu!" Jackson said.

C'mon, couldn't he shrivel up and die already? "Hey, Jackson."

"What were you saying?" Becca prompted.

She didn't seriously expect me to ask her in front of Jackson? And with the tool-belt-wielding sisters watching? With my luck, there were hidden cameras transmitting the event worldwide. But I couldn't turn back now. It was too late.

"I was wondering if you'd like to be in the show with me," I squeaked out in a voice that would have made a baby mouse proud.

Becca beamed in response. "Sure! Runway models! That sounds like fun."

"Whoa, that sounds cool," Jackson commented.

She looked back at him standing behind her.

"Oh, can Jackson be in the show, too?"

What? No! "Sure, of course. We need more models."

"Awesome!" Jackson exclaimed, giving me a high five. "Models in a fashion show!"

"Is anyone else going to be in it with us?" Becca asked.

The zombie warlord slumped down and began playing a funeral dirge using my intestines for bagpipes.

"I was going to ask Ben and Kirsten," I replied.

Becca's eyes lit up. "I'm gonna see Kirsten in a few minutes. If you want, I'll ask her for you."

"Sure."

The foursome hurried off down the sidewalk, two tittering about their new tool belts and two tittering about the show. At the corner, they turned and disappeared, leaving me standing in the middle of the sidewalk with my mouth gaping and my intestines still moaning.

What had just happened?

**42**

At least the conversation with my father went smoothly. Diane seemed relieved when I told her the news back at my grandmother's store.

"Thank the heavens," she said, peeking over the rack of dresses we were hiding behind. "Maybe it won't look like the Taj Mahal, but I'm sure it'll all pull together."

According to what Ben once told me, the Taj Mahal was built entirely of white marble. Comparing it to Harley's barn required a serious reach in logic. It'd be enough for me if people could walk across the floor without needing rubber boots or foot sanitizer.

My grandmother sauntered over, cane in hand, to our hiding spot.

"What are you two up to?" she asked.

"Oh, nothing," Diane replied. "Just sharing some town gossip."

My grandmother pursed her lips.

"You don't really seem like the gossip type. What else are you two conspiring about?"

The topic needed to change, quick. "I was just telling Diane I almost have the volunteers lined up for the show."

The zombie warlord resumed his slow dirge on my intestines.

"Well, that's good to hear. I'd like you all here tomorrow morning at ten a.m. to get fitted. Can you make that happen?"

"I think so. If it's okay, I'll leave early and talk to the last two on my way home."

My grandmother clapped me on the shoulder.

"I like your can-do attitude. Go ahead and take off. But make sure they're all here in the morning."

I marched to Ben's house and rapped on the front door. Instead of Ben yanking me inside,

Kirsten greeted me.

"Stu!" she exclaimed. "Becca stopped by and told us we're going to be runway models!"

Ben gave a fist bump.

"Yeah, you, me, Becca, Kirsten, and"—he gave me a questioning look—"Jackson."

He tilted his head to one side as if trying to solve the riddle of how Jackson came to be part of the mix. My own head had been stuck in that same position ever since Becca and Jackson strolled away together earlier.

"Yeah, about that . . ."

"It's all good," Kirsten beamed. She took Ben's hand and twirled. "We're going to be a smashing success prancing and twirling our way down the runway just like real fashion models."

"Real fashion models wearing old people clothes," Ben said.

"Actually," I explained. "This show is for everyone, and my grandmother wants to show off younger people's fashions, too."

"YES!" Kirsten and Ben shouted together.

"And also, some of the old people clothes won't fit on the other models."

"No worries," Ben replied, strutting about in a circle like a barnyard rooster. "We're going to make young people clothes *and* old people clothes look cool."

"You need to work on your cool," Kirsten observed, wagging her finger. "I'm not going up onstage with whatever you got going on there."

Ben stopped, his thrust-out chest deflating.

"Your words are hurting me."

Kirsten giggled.

"You know you're my little chicken," she teased.

My stomach lurched. It was time to get away from those two.

"Listen, my grandmother needs us at the store tomorrow morning to be fitted. Make sure you're there at ten a.m. sharp."

"Aye, aye, Captain," Ben said.

I skipped down the front steps before I had to witness any more of their baby talk. Just remembering the pet name *little chicken* brought on a dry heave. And I didn't dare look up as I passed Becca's steps. If I saw even a glimpse of Jackson, I was bound to bash my head against her retaining wall until either the wall or my head caved in.

And I was pretty sure it wouldn't be the wall.

# 43

My father didn't get home until almost midnight. He stumbled into my room yawning and carrying the remnants of the ham sandwich my mother had left in the fridge for him.

"You weren't kidding that Harley needed help," he said, plunking himself down on the corner of my bed. "There's layers of cow dung on that floor that go back generations."

The tiredness in his voice renewed my fears.

"Do you think the show will have to be canceled?" I asked.

He downed the glass of milk in his hand.

"No, I'm pretty sure with a little Truly ingenuity and a lot of backbreaking labor we'll find a way to have it ready in time. But for next year let's hope he gets an earlier start, like maybe in January."

I breathed a little sigh of relief.

"However," he continued, "we could use more help if you can roust up any of your friends the next couple nights."

Say what? "Do you mean to scoop poop?"

"Yes, there may be some poop-scooping involved." He grinned like a bleary-eyed diabolical genius. "But no need to bring that up when you're asking them."

Easy for him to say. It wasn't his friends being tricked into raking dried cow dung.

"Okay, I'll ask them tomorrow while we're being fitted. But I can't guarantee they'll agree to help. That barn is pretty gross."

My father finished his sandwich and headed to the door.

"What's with kids these days afraid to get their hands dirty with a little cow poop?" He paused. "On second thought: smart kids. Convince them anyway."

He closed the door and left me lying in bed wondering how long it would take to make new friends once my current ones realized they'd been tricked into forced labor poop-scooping. Probably a lifetime.

**44**

The next morning, I dragged myself into the store just as the wall clock flashed 10:00 a.m. Ben, Kirsten, Becca, and Jackson were already waiting in line to be fitted at my grandmother's sewing machine.

Elsa gave me a thumbs-up from her spot behind the counter. "Great job, Stu! Your grandmother is really pleased that you followed through on what she asked."

She pulled me behind the counter next to her.

"Though I'm still trying to figure out why there are five of you, not four."

Yeah, I was still trying to figure that out, too. "Well, Becca wanted Jackson in the show."

She gave me a puzzled look.

"Is that what *you* wanted?"

What I wanted involved a shark tank, a bloody bucket of chum, and a well-timed nudge to topple Jackson into the churning waters. "Not exactly."

"I see. Well, I respect your professionalism. And commitment to the show. I'm sure she'll come to her senses and realize in time that you're the real catch."

Apparently, Elsa hadn't seen his biceps, or my grades. On that cheery thought, I wandered over to the gang and waited my turn in line.

"Ben has to wear a suit," Kirsten giggled.

"At least I'm not the one wearing a tux with a ruffly shirt and everything," Ben countered.

Becca leaned over to me. "The three of us are going to model formal wear," she explained.

"Ruffly shirts are back in style," my grandmother added. "Aren't you the lucky ones."

Jackson pulled off his T-shirt revealing pec muscles and actual abs that could be individually counted.

"I don't mind. I like ruffly shirts."

He pulled on a white tux shirt with ruffles running up and down the chest and around both cuffs.

"Looks good on you," Kirsten commented.

If I had a handful of sharks, I'd show her what looked good on him.

"Stu, try this on," my grandmother said, handing me a black tux jacket with satin trim.

My fingertips barely poked out of the sleeves.

"Looks like it's going to need some altering," my grandmother observed.

"Or maybe you could just give him hand puppets to hold," Ben quipped. "You know, like turtles or baby chicks peeking out of each sleeve."

That brought about a lot more giggling than seemed necessary.

"Shut up." Honestly, how did I get stuck with that guy for a best friend?

After we finished being measured, marked, and fitted, I walked the four of them outside. It was time for the other invitation. The one that involved less fashion and more stinky poop-scooping.

"Hey, my dad was hoping we could all come over to Harley's the next couple evenings and help get the barn ready."

"Sure," Kirsten said. "What does he want us to do?"

Now for the delicate part. How to convince them that raking muck was a fun group activity.

"I don't know. Just pick up stuff, and stuff."

That seemed clear enough for me.

"Sure," Ben said.

"I'm in," Jackson agreed.

"Us too," Becca finished.

"And I know who else will be happy to help," Ben added.

We grinned at each other the way we always grinned right before getting our two closest friends into something they'd regret.

"Tyler and Ryan!"

Of course.

**45**

That evening all seven of us gathered along with the meat float crew outside Harley's barn. From the looks they kept giving us, I wondered if maybe I should have been more specific about what to wear. Kirsten had on white shorts and a yellow top. Becca wore sandals. And Jackson had on khaki pants and a button-up pink shirt that proved at least some guys can wear pink and still look studly.

On the other hand, the meat float crew had on rubber boots, muck-worthy shirts and pants, and leather gloves. Clearly, they had been in battle the night before and had come dressed for the next skirmish. My father exited the barn and addressed the troops.

"Okay," my father began. "We have some new recruits this evening."

"They look ready to muck," Joe commented.

That brought a round of laughter from the meat float crew. My father held up a hand.

"Yes, some of you look better suited for work outside the barn."

He pointed to Kirsten, Becca, and Jackson.

"How about you three start in the front yard. Anything you find that doesn't belong there put in a wheelbarrow and then throw it all into the back of my truck and I'll take it to the dump tomorrow. There are extra gloves on the seat of the truck. I suggest you wear them."

"And if it moves, don't touch it," Joe added with a snort.

Becca and Kirsten gave each other disgusted looks, then broke into smiles.

"Yes, sir," Kirsten said, saluting. "We'll get right on it."

My father turned his attention to Ben, Tyler, Ryan, and me.

"The rest of you grab a rake or shovel and follow us. We'll show you what to do."

"Aren't you the lucky ones!" Joe added.

We followed the men into the barn and got a quick lesson in cleaning up cow manure.

"Just rake it onto a shovel, then throw it into this wheelbarrow," Joe explained. "When it's full, wheel it out and dump it into my trailer. When the trailer's full, it's time to go home."

We peeked out at Joe's trailer, it looked big enough to haul a mountain of muck.

"You didn't mention we were going to be picking up cow poop," Ben whispered.

"Yeah, I thought we were going to hang out and have fun," Ryan added.

C'mon, really? Even I wasn't that gullible. "We're here to help clean up Harley's barn. What did you think we were going to do?"

Tyler looked as if he had just now realized he was standing inside a dilapidated old barn.

"I don't know. Build hay forts and stuff."

Now that's what I call naive.

After what seemed like days, we reached the far corner and stretched our aching backs. Behind us lay a ragged surface full of scrape marks and missing chunks of dirt.

"It's not exactly a thing of beauty," Harley remarked.

"No," my father agreed. "It needs a steamroller to smooth things out."

"Or landscaping bark to cover it up," Joe suggested.

My father rested his head on the handle of his shovel and sighed. "Yeah, I think you're right."

Joe nodded. "I can have it here tomorrow evening."

"I've got a piano lesson tomorrow night," Ryan whined on the way home.

"Me too," Ben agreed.

"You don't play the piano," I reminded him.

Ben took a whiff of his own armpit.

"Anything to get out of doing that again."

Tyler held his hands out in front of him as if afraid they might touch something, like his own body.

"I think I'd even take up square dancing again," he said. "If it meant not having to go back to that barn."

I had to admit the last couple hours had been pretty much the most disgusting thing I'd ever done. And I'm not even talking about scooping poop. Every time I looked outside, I had to watch Jackson skipping through the grass within hand-holding length of Becca while they searched for junk to pick up. Where were man-eating sharks when I needed them?

**46**

The next night, we made our final assault on the barn floor shoveling landscaping bark in to replace the muck we had shoveled out. It was still hard work but a lot better smelling than the night before. Plus, Jackson had a church youth group meeting and couldn't join us. That in and of itself made the night far more enjoyable. Ryan and Tyler also bagged out with the unlikely excuse that they had been grounded, though I knew full well they were hanging out at Tyler's house playing video games.

That left Kirsten, Becca, Ben, and me to carry on without them.

"This is hard work," Kirsten remarked ten minutes later.

"That's what I've been telling ya," Ben said, wheeling in another load.

"We're just like real farmers," Becca said.

Ben dumped the load at our feet.

"Yeah, beauty bark farmers," he joked.

"Better than farming cow manure," I countered.

"True," he agreed, wrinkling his nose. "No more manure for me, ever."

Becca flexed her biceps.

"I'm getting pretty ripped," she proclaimed.

I flexed my own biceps. Despite the dim light, an actual bulge could be seen through the sleeve of my T-shirt. Mind you a small bulge that required magnification to verify, but a bulge nonetheless. Hey, maybe all this shoveling had paid off.

"Whoa, you got guns, boy," Kirsten said.

Becca put her arm up next to mine.

"Who's got guns?" she said.

Frankly, it was hard to say who had the bigger guns. Not that I felt in any way embarrassed by that fact. I'm a modern man, right? I changed my pose to look like an emaciated version of the Incredible Hulk.

"Yeah, well, look at all this hugeness," I said, trembling with effort.

Becca followed my example and did her best Hulk impression, followed by Kirsten and, lastly, Ben. He outdid us all by being able to make actual veins bulge out on his neck.

"Ooh, look at that," Kirsten said, pointing.

"Wicked," Becca added. "I hope one of them doesn't explode."

Funny. I was hoping just the opposite.

The next two hours went by in a blur of laughter and general silliness as we continued to sprinkle beauty bark while striking body builder poses. Even my father and his buddies started posing during their breaks.

"Now, this is what the Hulk should really look like," Joe said, contorting his body until he looked like a flexing panda bear.

"Okay, everybody," my father called as he threw a last shovel of bark. "I think that does it. Time to call it a night."

"Thanks, everyone," Harley said as he shook each of

our hands. "I don't know how I could have done this without you."

Two nights of physical labor hit me like a load of dried manure when I got home. My arms couldn't even lift the second sandwich my mother had left out. And yet I felt better than I had in a long time. Spending time with Becca without Jackson hovering around reminded me what it had been like in the old days, back when we went on a single movie date together and on a single family picnic. Had our relationship really been that short-lived?

I pulled out my notebook and pen. Maybe there was still hope. Maybe this time I could find the words to write an epic poem expressing my feelings. Maybe I could win her back yet.

I relaxed my mind. And let the ballpoint tip of the pen rest on the page. Trust your feelings, Stu. It had worked for Luke Skywalker in *Star Wars*—why not me? Creative energy swirled inside my brain until I could feel a stream of words building like floodwaters ready to burst over the dammed wall of my own awkwardness.

*Speak to her*, the voice in my head said. Speak from

the heart. Speak the words you long to tell her without fear of embarrassment, or the thought of what might happen if Ben sees them.

I tried to keep my focus, but the moment slipped away until I found myself staring at the Seattle Sounders poster taped on my wall. I gently set down my pen, closed the notebook, and threw it in the trash.

So much for being a poet.

**47**

The next two days at the store went by in a blur of pre-show panic.

"The U-Haul dealer forgot about our reservation and doesn't have any rental trucks available this weekend. How are we supposed to move all the clothes?" Elsa moaned from behind the counter.

"There won't be any need," my grandmother added from behind the mountain of clothes piled around her sewing machine, "if I don't get all the alterations finished in time."

Diane paced back and forth like a nervous woman looking for reasons to be nervous. "It all comes down to now, doesn't it?" she babbled to herself. "This is why I left show business. Too much stress, too much craziness, too little time."

"STU!" all three ladies yelled at once. "I need your help!"

Somehow, I stayed calm, cool, and collected while feverishly sorting, hanging, and bagging the finished clothes. By Friday afternoon, we were all huffing from exhaustion.

"We did it!" Diane exclaimed.

"Every year it's a race to the finish," my grandmother explained.

"An even bigger race this year with twice the number of models," Elsa added.

I had to admit it had been a thrill ride. Not quite like the Zipper but better than shoveling cow poop.

On my way home, a rumble brought my attention to Harley on his bike. He pulled up next to me and held out his spare helmet.

"Hey, dude, get on."

"I'm not supposed to ride with you."

He gave a Harley-sized grin. "No worries. I got it all worked out with your mom. You can ride with me now."

"Cool! Where are we going?" I asked, pulling on the helmet.

"To my place."

For the second time in months, I clung to Harley as we roared out of town. This time I forced my head to the side so I could see the world whizzing past. Fields and pastures and farm houses blurred into shades of purple and green that somehow seemed more vibrant when viewed from a rumbling two-wheeled death machine. It was like a carnival thrill ride but without the childish screams and vomit smells.

Unfortunately, the ride only lasted a few minutes before we chugged into Harley's driveway and came to a stop next to his barn. He took my helmet and dropped it next to his on the grass.

"I don't want Elsa to see the barn until it's all done," he said. "But I wanted to show someone before I put on the finishing touches."

We crossed to the barn, and Harley pulled open the two massive sliding doors.

"Um . . . it looks nice," I said, peering into the darkness.

He frowned at the hesitation in my voice.

"Hang on a minute. The show is just getting started."

He guided me over to where a trailer with what looked like a car engine had been parked next to the barn. He flipped a couple switches, then yanked a pull cord.

"The electric panel for the house wasn't big enough so I brought in a gas-powered generator to add lighting to the main part of the barn," he yelled over the roar of the engine.

I walked back and peeked through the barn doors again. Lights hanging from the rafters lit up every inch of the interior, which suddenly seemed like a bad idea. The new lighting revealed the barn in all its naked glory. By *glory* I mean decrepit, skanky, falling-down glory. The graying wood walls bowed out as if the barn were slowly sinking to its knees. Cobwebs hung everywhere. A single rat stared from its perch on one of the rafters.

"I still got a bit to do to get it ready for guests," Harley said.

A bit to do? Did bulldozing and building a new barn count as a bit? How had I not noticed before what an ugly old barn Harley owned?

He guided me to his workshop and swung open the door to reveal the next chamber in his house of horrors. A wooden divider split the room in half. His sculptures had been lined up along the walls and jammed around his workbench. There was barely enough room left for more than a couple people to undress without colliding. All in all, it looked like a perfect bunk room for miniature-sized cowboys, but not for adult-sized models changing clothes during the show. How they and their clothes would fit would take a Christmas miracle.

"Nice, huh?" he said. "Separate changing areas for the guys and gals."

"Uh, yeah."

He grabbed my shoulder.

"Oh, I almost forgot. There's one more thing you gotta see."

He led the way out of the barn and around the corner to an open area between the building and an unused pasture. The ground had been scraped bare in a perfect rectangle.

"This is where the Honey Buckets are going to be lined up."

"The what?"

Harley clapped me on the back.

"You know, the porta potties that people can use when they need to go to the bathroom. There will be a whole row of them right here. I made sure it was a location downwind from the barn. Don't need any unwanted smells wafting in during the show," he said with a laugh.

A sinking feeling pulled my stomach down to my knees. It had been my idea to move the show to Harley's. What had I done? The image of people in suits and gowns traipsing about a collapsing barn filled with rats and without indoor plumbing made my stomach squeeze tight. How could I have been so stupid? Don't get me wrong, Harley was the person I'd most like to be when I grew up, but the idea of him hosting a fashion show in his moldy old barn suddenly seemed beyond crazy. I understood now why my grandmother and Diane had been against it. They must have been out of their minds trusting me and the handlebar-mustached rebel without a clue standing next to me.

"So, what do you think?" Harley asked.

I think our only hope was to torch the place and use the insurance money to buy a used circus tent. "Looks great."

His shoulders visibly relaxed.

"I've been a bit worried about whether I could have it ready in time," he admitted. "There's still a lot to do, but now that the hardest parts are done, I can relax a little."

The last thing he needed was to relax. Sometimes panic is a good thing. Especially when you have one day left and a new barn to build. "That's good."

I lay in bed that night reviewing the evening's revelations. Harley's barn looked like a frontier house of horrors. The models would only be able to change if they stood on top of each other. And if the sights and smells proved to be too much, guests could retreat to a Honey Bucket and spend a few minutes relaxing on a plastic toilet seat suspended above a pit of raw sewage.

It was time to admit the truth: the show was doomed.

I arrived at the store the next morning with the weight
of the world wrapped around me like a Darth Vader
cloak.

"Hey, Stu," Elsa bubbled as I entered. "Can you
believe the show is today?"

Nope. Harley needed at least another century to
have his barn ready, possibly a full millennium. "Yeah,
exciting, huh?"

She literally twirled with excitement.

"The town is buzzing! Seems like everyone is coming. Several of the restaurants are hosting special
brunches before the show. And did your grandmother
tell you we're sold out of formal gowns? And Stefan's
store sold out of suits. It's becoming the social event of

the season. The day is going to be AMAZING!"

Oh, it was going to be amazing, all right. Barn-collapsing, rat-swarming, Honey Bucket–dripping amazing. "Yeah, can't wait."

"Harley told me he took you out to his place last night. How did it look?"

Her eyes were so excited, and so sincere. What was I supposed to say? "Great. Looks great."

"Oh, I'm so glad! It's all coming together beautifully!"

My grandmother arrived, followed by Diane and company.

"Stu, good to see you," my grandmother said. "And I hear you've been out to Harley's."

Not her, too. How much longer could I hide the truth about the disaster-in-the-making brewing at his barn? "Yeah, it's looking good."

Apparently, at least a little bit longer.

"Good to hear. We're counting on him coming through for us today."

Yeah, about that.

"Well," I started, "he's been working nonstop to get ready." That much was true. "But it won't be the Taj Mahal." I think that summed things up pretty well.

My grandmother brushed off the last sentence with a shrug.

"At this point, as long as it holds everyone and doesn't fall down, I think the show will be a smashing success."

Oh, it was going to be smashing, that was for sure.

We went to work loading the clothes into the U-Haul truck my father had scrounged along with all manner of accessories including tape, scissors, an iron, safety pins, and even my grandmother's sewing machine.

"You never know when a seam is going to tear apart at the last moment," my grandmother explained.

By noon, everything was loaded, checked, rechecked, and, at last, ready to go.

"There will be plenty of help unloading at Harley's," Elsa said. "And your mom is meeting us there to set up the changing area. Why don't you go round up your troops and make sure everyone is there no later than two p.m.?"

Really? I didn't have to be there when they saw Harley's barn? Maybe their desire to strangle me would have cooled off by the time I arrived.

"Hey, dude," Ben said when I showed up on his doorstep. "You're early. Everyone else won't be here for at least an hour."

"Perfect," I replied, helping myself to the sandwich he was holding. "I'm starving, and I need a break before we head to the show."

Ben poured a couple glasses of lemonade and motioned for me to take a seat on the couch. He piled a mound of Oreos on another plate and slouched down next to me.

"It's going to be pretty awesome," he said, spraying chunks of Oreo out of his mouth like Cookie Monster on *Sesame Street*.

"What?"

"The show."

"Oh yeah, except for when the barn falls down."

"Maybe they can give everybody hard hats to wear during the show."

An Oreo chunk landed in my lap.

"Or maybe we can all wear Iron Man suits," I suggested. "That'd be pretty cool."

I flicked the chunk off and grabbed the last cookie off the plate.

"Yeah! That's it!" Ben agreed. "We can all wear Iron Man suits and after the show we can fly around and fire rockets at each other."

I shoved the last cookie into my mouth. "If only we had a couple hundred Iron Man suits."

"Or at least rockets."

"I'll see what I can do."

Ben downed the rest of his lemonade.

"You may want an Iron Man suit to hide in when you walk down the runway with Becca—and Jackson."

"Shut up."

"Seriously, how's that gonna work?" Ben asked.

"Seriously, I don't know. Maybe he'll accidentally fall off the stage and break a leg or something."

"That'd be cool." Ben scratched his chin. "The thing is, I don't even dislike the guy."

I couldn't help but nod. "I know. There's nothing worse than being friends with the guy you hate."

"For real. I still hope he breaks his leg, though."

"Me too."

Ben carried the plates into the kitchen and dumped them in the sink.

"You going to Becca's party?"

Leave it to Ben to bring up the thing I'd been avoiding thinking about.

"Don't suppose she canceled it?"

"Nope."

Dang, so much for hope.

"I don't know. I guess so."

"What did you get her?"

"Nothing yet."

He giggled, but not the funny sort of giggle.

"Dude, you are the worst boyfriend ever."

"Shut up. I'm not even her boyfriend."

He shook his head.

"Dude, your life is messed up."

He had that right.

**49**

Becca, Kirsten, and Jackson arrived right at 1:30. They took turns making a grand entrance as if the entryway were a catwalk.

"Do I intrigue you?" Kirsten said, striding past with haughty coolness.

"Do I defy you?" Becca purred through pouty lips.

"Do I destroy you?" Jackson added, subtly flexing his biceps as he joined them in the living room.

Ben bounced out the door, then took his turn making an entrance.

"Do I disgust you?" he said, posing with his shirt unbuttoned.

Not to be outdone, I exited, before reentering with my own shirt unbuttoned.

"Does he *still* disgust you?" I said, posing next to Ben. We all broke into giggles.

"This is going to be awesome!" Kirsten exclaimed.

"We're going to rock the show," Ben agreed.

"Heaven help us," Ben's mother said, entering. She waved us to follow her out to her SUV.

The ride gave me time to think about what lay ahead. And time for the horde of butterflies in my stomach to whip up my stomach acid into a nervous froth. For starters, everyone was bound to hate the barn and, in turn, the fool who suggested it. On top of that, I would most likely be forced to follow behind Becca and Jackson on the runway like their grumpy stepchild. And to top things off, as soon as the show ended, I'd be forced to attend Becca's birthday party and publicly admit that the only present I had brought was the sound of my hand slapping my own forehead.

"Everything okay?" Becca asked as we turned into Harley's driveway.

Perfect. Never better.

We stepped out of the SUV into a swarm of activity. Workers carried white folding chairs into the barn from the back of a truck. More workers set up little tables dotting the courtyard outside the barn. A catering truck unloaded shiny metal serving trays and white tablecloths onto long tables rowed next to their truck. And a group of teens were being given instructions how to direct cars into the parking area behind Harley's house.

"Hey, glad you made it," Harley said, crossing from the barn to greet us.

His demeanor seemed chipper, but he had circles under his eyes and he was wearing the same clothes I'd seen him in last evening.

"How are you holding up?" Ben's mom asked.

Harley gave her a tired grin.

"Well, things took a little longer than I expected. Kinda stayed up all night to get everything done." He ran a hand through his greasy hair. "But it seems all good now."

Elsa trotted up and patted Harley's back.

"Wait till you see what he did," she said, beaming. "He's such an artist."

So far, things weren't going at all like I'd expected. Elsa was grinning. And no one yet had attempted to strangle me. Maybe the afternoon held hope yet.

Elsa ushered us to the barn. On the way, she gave us an overview of what we were seeing.

"The caterer is setting up over there," she said, pointing. "They are going to have meat and cheese plates, steak skewers, artichoke dip, and a vegetable medley that is simply divine."

Her arm swung to the tables dotting the barn's entry.

"The tables are for people to eat before or during the show. They'll be covered in white satin tablecloths with folding chairs for seating."

She stopped before we reached the barn doors and gathered us close in a conspiratorial huddle.

"But the real surprise will be when people enter the barn." She spread both arms like a circus showman. "Behold this year's fall fashion show venue!"

She stepped aside and motioned us forward. The moment our eyes adjusted to the dim light we gasped.

The overhead lighting had been removed. In its place strings of dangling lights hung from the rafters, twinkling like tiny stars in the celestial barnyard heavens. Along the back wall of the barn a runway had been constructed with a center section that extended through the middle of the barn, allowing the models to walk out into the crowd. Rows of white folding chairs filled the areas on either side of the runway. And around the perimeter of the barn, Harley's sculptures had been placed, each lit from beneath so that they glowed like mythical sentinels guarding the show. Harley had been busy since I left, inhumanly busy.

"It's beautiful," Kirsten whispered.

"Like a fairy wonderland," Becca added.

"So cool," Jackson agreed.

"Dude!" Ben said, punching my arm.

Whatever concerns I'd had about the barn melted away. Harley was a genius. How had I ever doubted him?

"Stu!" my grandmother called from the stage. "You're here just in time. The models are about to get a modeling lesson from my good friend Aruna."

We joined the gang of other models including Diane and company and the meat float crew. My grandmother directed our attention to the dark-haired woman standing beside her on the stage.

"As I was saying, Aruna owns Northwest Modeling and agreed to help out by giving you all a modeling lesson before the show. Please give my dear friend your undivided attention."

Aruna stepped forward with her hand outstretched in a gesture of welcome. Despite looking about the same age as my grandmother, her every movement held the graceful precision of a ballerina and her skin glowed a deep orangey brown as if she had just arrived from some faraway tropical kingdom.

"I'm honored to be here today," she said. "And to give you a quick lesson in runway modeling."

"She's beautiful," Becca whispered.

Aruna strode a few steps down the runway, then turned back.

"If you can remember these three tips, you'll do

great today," she said. "First, think tall as you walk. Second, keep your eyes forward. And third, have a little attitude, but also have fun with it."

She strutted back looking every bit like a real runway model.

"Well, at least I can do the third one," Joe commented.

Aruna brought us up onstage. We formed a line, then took turns walking the catwalk. It was one thing to talk about being a model. But completely different to actually walk down a runway trying to keep your cool. Especially when your cool lacked a few things like cool hair, cool biceps, or cool gorilla-strength antiperspirant.

My first turn on the catwalk looked more like an inmate on death row heading to the electric chair.

"Try relaxing your shoulders," Aruna prompted. "And let your arms swing freely. And show a little attitude."

Frankly, it took all my attitude to even be up on the stage.

"Like this?" I said, yanking my shoulders down and forcing my arms away from my sides.

She gave my grandmother a thin-lipped smile.

"Yes, better. A little more relaxed would be great."

Yeah, right. I could already feel the crowd's eyes boring holes into me and there wasn't even a crowd yet.

At last, the lesson ended, and we took a break for some much-needed fresh air. A line of cars stretched out of Harley's driveway and around the corner of the road. Couples of all ages in suits and gowns milled about the catering truck or stood gaping at the interior of the barn.

"That was awesome!" Ben said, beaming like a modeling idiot.

"Yeah, we're gonna work the crowd into a frenzy," Kirsten said, beaming just like Ben.

Easy for them to say. They hadn't broken their nose square dancing in front of the whole school. I excused myself from the group and sauntered over to one of the Honey Buckets to settle my nerves. Being trapped in the stinky compartment in no way helped. After a few minutes, I staggered back outside. And that's when I discovered Diane pacing behind the Honey Buckets looking pale and a little green.

"You okay?" I asked.

"I'm not sure I can go through with this," she moaned, dabbing at one eye. "I'm not built to be a model."

"Me neither," I agreed. "I was freaking out just doing the practice runs."

"Really?" she asked.

"Yeah, the last time I had to be up in front of people I broke my nose and bled all over my dance partner."

"No wonder you're nervous," she consoled. "And I thought I had reason to be scared."

"What do we do?"

She wrapped an arm around me and squeezed.

"I don't know. Just keep going, I guess. Just keep going."

50

Just before showtime, Elsa ushered us into the dressing room. With Harley's artwork removed, it had enough space to fit everyone, so long as we gave Joe one end to himself. Even with the door shut the noise of the crowd buzzed around us.

"The crowd's even bigger than we expected," Elsa said, gathering us around. "During the show, I'll be at the door calling out who's up next. Make sure you're ready when it's your turn."

The first song of the evening started up, and a loud disco beat vibrated the walls.

"That's the cue for everyone to take a seat," Elsa explained. "Get changed and be ready to go."

The zombie warlord in my chest banged out an urgent message in Morse code: A-A-A-H-H-H-H-H-!-!

R-U-N A-W-A-Y-!-!-! Exactly. Except where was I supposed to go? Not to mention Ben had me in a headlock.

"Don't even think about it!" he shouted over the
music.

Reluctantly, I let go of the door handle.

"I just wanted to peek out," I lied.

"In your underwear?"

He had a point. I should have freaked out before
starting to undress.

"Oh, all right. You can let go of me."

Ben released his grip, and I slunk back to the rack
of clothes with my name on it. My first outfit consisted
of corduroy pants, a button-down denim shirt, and a
lightweight leather jacket slung over one shoulder. Not
too scary, right?

"Becca, Jackson, and Stu, you're up," Elsa called out.

WHAT? My pits started spewing sweat like a spastic
sprinkler. Jackson grabbed my arm and pulled me over
to where Becca waited next to Elsa.

"Here's the deal," Elsa whispered. "As soon as the
next song starts, that's your cue." She motioned to
Jackson. "You lead the way. Becca will be next. And

then Stu. Once you reach the center catwalk, walk in unison to the end and back." She gave us a thumbs-up. "And give 'em a little attitude!"

For one long moment, the music stopped. And then a new song began. It started quietly before building into a throbbing dance rhythm. Elsa opened the door and nodded.

"It's go time!"

We shuffled to the base of the stage steps behind a black screen that kept us hidden from the crowd.

"Let's do it!" Jackson whispered, tugging us forward.

And that's when I froze.

"What's wrong?" Becca asked.

If I thought I had been nervous during our practice, it was nothing to the adrenaline pumping through my body now. Any moment, I expected my insides to spontaneously combust like a faulty Fourth of July rocket and explode in a burst of bloody glory that would end the show before it even started.

"I—I can't do it."

Jackson pulled harder on Becca's hand.

"C'mon, we gotta go."

Becca slipped her hand from Jackson's and turned to me.

"Stu, what's wrong?"

"I'm—no good—at this," I stammered. "I'm terrible onstage, and—and—" What was the word I was searching for? "I'm spindly."

Had I just used the word *spindly*?

Becca squeezed my hand and gave me a look so sincere I actually believed it.

"You're not spindly." She broke into a grin. "And anyway, spindly is the new studly! Didn't you know?"

As a matter of fact, I didn't. But in that moment, staring into her eyes glittering with sincerity, I would have believed anything, even the pile of cow poop she had just spewed. Her hand pulled me forward. The zombie warlord gave a groan and slumped down.

Together, we climbed the steps to stardom.

**51**

Okay, maybe stardom was an overstatement. But the crowd genuinely cheered when we took the stage. We sauntered side by side down the length of the catwalk into the sea of faces. Beside me, Jackson and Becca looked pretty much like you'd expect: all glam and attitude all the time.

Despite my legs trembling, I found enough inner swagger to relax my shoulders and let my arms swing freely, almost like Aruna had demonstrated.

At the end of the catwalk, we turned and paused, dismissing the audience with our hip cool. And then we strolled back without missing a beat despite the hoots and hollers shouted in our wake.

"You guys were awesome!" Elsa gushed when we entered the dressing room. "You're naturals!"

"Dude!" Ben exclaimed. "You the man!"

I gave him a high five as he and Kirsten headed for their turn on the catwalk.

"You're almost a man, too!" I encouraged.

Not like he needed any extra encouragement. His chest was already so inflated I worried he'd float off the stage into the rafters.

Diane peeked around the corner of the dressing divider and motioned me over.

"How did you do it?" she asked.

"I don't know. Like you said I guess—I just kept going."

I could see her knuckles turning white. Without thinking, I patted her hand.

"And anyway, everyone here *loves* you."

"Diane, you're up," Elsa called.

She dabbed at an eye, then gave me a hug.

"Stu, you are an amazing young man. Thank you."

With a parting wave, she disappeared through the doorway to the catwalk.

Even from backstage, I could hear the reception reserved just for Diane. The crowd exploded into cheers when she took the stage and didn't stop cheering until she breezed back into the dressing room looking like the old Diane.

"That was amazing!" she gushed. "I had no idea the crowd would be so kind!"

"Really?" I asked. "You're pretty much a rock star wherever you go."

She swept me under one wing.

"You make me wish I'd had kids. And that's saying something."

Onstage the show continued to be a lovefest between the models and the audience, with the occasional heckle thrown in for fun such as "Hey, Joe, will you be my lamb chop?"—a clear reference to his meat float costume. And "Hey, Stu, nice ruffly shirt!" a clear reference to why Ryan and Tyler should have been banned from attending.

After an hour of prancing and preening, Elsa, at last, called us together backstage for a few final instructions.

"You guys have been SO AMAZING! All that's left is to take a final bow."

A disappointed groan went up from the group. Elsa grinned.

"You'll be going up onstage one couple at a time with Diane and Joe at the lead. Spread out until you fill the entire center stage. When the music stops, Rosemarie is going to say a few words and then you're all going to take a final bow. And that'll be the end of the show!"

A high-energy pop beat pulsed through the barn and got the audience clapping in unison with the beat.

"This is it!" Kirsten exclaimed.

"Our last chance to rock the stadium," Ben added.

Jackson slid over next to me.

"Hey, Stu, I really appreciate you letting me be part of the show. But I kinda crashed the party. I'm gonna sit this one out."

He nodded toward Becca.

"You two go without me."

Seriously? Yes! Finally! For once, it would be just Becca and me onstage together without a bicep-flexing, ab-rippling, lone-chin-hair-wielding creature from the deep stealing the limelight.

From behind one of his brawny shoulders, Becca

peeked over at me. Okay, so Jackson hadn't done one thing all evening to steal the limelight. He had just been himself. And frankly the audience loved him, especially the girls in attendance under the age of sixty. It wasn't his fault he had been born a muscle-bound stud.

"No, you should come up onstage with us. We've been a team all night. We gotta see it through to the end."

"Dude, you're right," he replied, clapping my shoulder. "We're Team Stu."

He broke into a smile. Which did little to comfort me. But next to him Becca also smiled.

"Team Stu!" she repeated.

Oh, why not. Go, Team Stu!

## 52

We climbed onstage one last time and took our places spread out along the center runway while the crowd clapped and cheered. At last, the music stopped. And my grandmother, followed by Stefan and Elsa, walked to the end of the runway. She held up a microphone and addressed the crowd.

"Wow. Has this been fun, or what?"

A chorus of whistles and cheers erupted.

"Thank you all so much for coming out today in support of the show."

More cheers.

"I want to take a moment and thank a few people who made today possible."

She motioned Stefan to join her.

"First, a big thank-you to the man standing next to

me, who agreed to join forces this year in making this our first-ever coed fashion show. Thank you, Stefan! And I hope all you men in the audience will make Town and Country the store for all your clothing needs."

A big round of applause went up as Stefan took a gracious bow.

"Next," my grandmother continued, "I want to recognize all the hours of work put in by my lovely, talented, and capable store manager Elsa. Without her energy and dedication this show would not have happened."

An even bigger round of applause greeted Elsa as she curtsied, her cheeks glowing bright red. My grandmother raised one hand to quiet the crowd.

"As many of you know, we lost our venue a week ago due to a most unfortunate electrical fire. Just when the show seemed doomed, my grandson had the foresight and courage to save the day. Thank you, Stu!"

A wall of noise roared from the crowd. My ears turned the color of Elsa's cheeks.

"You the man!" Ben yelled into my ear. "Show 'em your guns!"

I gave a weak wave to the audience. From the corner

of my eye, I could see Becca and Kirsten giggling together. Okay, maybe spindly was a little bit studly. Right?

My grandmother waved the crowd to silence again.

"There's one man who truly saved the day for us. One man who stepped up to help when all seemed lost and who gave an entire week of his life to make this the most amazing fashion show venue ever. His artwork is all around you and he never ceases to amaze me with his talent and kindness."

She paused for effect.

"Harley? Where are you? Come up onstage!"

From the back of the crowd, a mountain of a man with a greasy mustache and black vest walked forward. He looked like something out of a spaghetti Western, a man beyond mere mortal men. A chant went up from the crowd: "Har-ley, Har-ley, Har-ley!"

He reached the stage and hopped up without missing a beat.

"Har-ley, Har-ley, Har-ley!" the crowd continued.

"Sounds like he doesn't need any introduction," my

grandmother said. "Thank you, Harley, for everything!"

Suddenly, Elsa threw her arms around Harley and kissed him right there in front of everyone. A collective gasp went through the crowd. And then everyone went wild cheering.

"Go, Harley!" someone shouted.

"You the man!" another screamed. Okay, that might have been me. But it was still true.

Finally, my grandmother waved her arms for quiet.

"There's one more thank-you I want to give. For the first time we didn't use professional models. Instead, we approached people in the community. People who had never done anything like this before. And frankly, who were pretty nervous about strutting out onstage in front of you all. But they were good sports. And I think you'll agree that they were fabulous models."

She swept a hand around her at all the models.

"Please join me in giving them a big round of applause!"

The audience gave a standing ovation that lasted for what must have been minutes. Some of the models hugged or blew kisses to the crowd. Ben, Kirsten, Jackson, Becca, and I high-fived each other. Diane dabbed at both eyes while Joe hugged her shoulders.

At last, the crowd headed for the exit doors. Harley came over and gave me a fist bump.

"You were a stud up there on the catwalk," he said.

Elsa joined us, her cheeks still flushed.

"Thanks for helping arrange things the way you did," she said.

Harley wrapped an arm around her.

"Seems like it all worked out," I replied, giving them my you-know-what-I-mean look.

They both grinned like middle schoolers at a middle school dance.

"Yeah," they agreed.

"Hey, Stu!" my mother called from across the barn. "Your friends are waiting. Time to leave for Becca's party."

Party? What party? Oh, chipotle.

**53**

I found Becca waiting next to her parents' SUV.

"C'mon," she insisted. "My dad's waiting for us at the park."

She took the seat up front next to her mom. Ben and Kirsten had the middle seats, leaving me in the back with Jackson and Carly. Carly immediately scooted over next to Jackson.

"I'm sitting with you," she announced, looking up at him with eager eyes. The same eyes that refused to acknowledge me sitting on her other side.

The car ride gave me plenty of time to note the wrapped presents on everyone's laps. Everyone's laps except mine. Where they had hidden them during the show I couldn't guess. It was like magic. The sort of magic that makes some people look like perfect friends while making others look like perfect idiots.

"Where's your present?" Carly asked.

Well, at least she wasn't ignoring me.

"Um, well, it's a long story," I replied, keeping my voice low.

"Do you *have* a present?"

There's nothing worse than being humiliated by someone half your age. "Well, not in the traditional sense." Whatever that meant.

"All *my* friends brought presents when *I* had a party."

"That's nice."

We finally pulled into Sequim Bay State Park and followed a paved drive that wound through dozens of picnic sites. The park would make a perfect place for a horror film with all its towering evergreen trees casting shadows everywhere. Perfect for frightening movie viewers. Or the only guy at a birthday party without a present.

Becca's mom pulled into a parking space next to the picnic table where Becca's dad had set up camp.

"Oh, look," Kirsten exclaimed. "He's already got a fire going."

"Yes," Becca's mom agreed. "It gets cool at night in the woods this close to the water. The bay is just a short hike through the trees."

We piled out and greeted the other handful of partygoers including Tyler, Ryan, Gretchen, Annie, and Lisa. Together we huddled around the fire while Becca's parents finished laying out food on the picnic table. Becca's mom had been right. It did get cool quick here at night.

"Okay, everyone," she called. "Lots of choices here including both regular and meatless hot dogs, potato chips, a veggie tray, fruit, and lemonade to drink. Come help yourselves."

After a hard afternoon of modeling, Ben and I piled our plates with food.

"These meatless hot dogs are pretty good," Ben commented between mouthfuls.

"You're holding a carrot stick," Becca clarified.

He stared at the carrot in his hand. "Oh, that explains why it tastes like a carrot."

That got a few giggles. I refused to support such forced humor. Especially since I hadn't thought of it first.

After dinner, Becca's dad brought out sticks and marshmallows to roast while Becca's mom laid out chocolate bars and graham crackers for s'mores.

"Have at it," she said.

Ryan and Tyler immediately went into action.

"We'll show you how it's done," Tyler said, piercing a marshmallow with the tip of his roasting stick.

We all watched as they demonstrated the proper technique to hover the stick near the flames until the marshmallow toasted golden brown. Except it never worked out like that. Tyler's marshmallow caught on fire and charred black before he could blow out the flames. Ryan's marshmallow slid off the end of his stick and tumbled between two of the logs, where it slowly oozed and bubbled until there was nothing left but a charred blob of goo.

After that, everyone grabbed a stick and attempted to toast the perfect marshmallow. Mostly, we caught

them on fire and waved them around like goopy spar-
klers. Then we slid the charred remains onto a graham
cracker, added a piece of chocolate, layered another
graham cracker on top, then crammed the gooey sweet
sandwiches into our mouths.

"This is heaven," Ben exclaimed between mouthfuls.

"Divine," Kirsten agreed.

"I lost another one in the fire," Ryan added.

Yep. That sounded about right. With the focus on
s'more building, I began to hold out hope I'd get lucky
and we'd run out of time before anyone remembered
the pile of presents lying next to the picnic table.

"Time for presents," Lisa suggested, holding hers up
for all to see.

So much for luck.

Everyone trooped over and retrieved their gift off
the pile. Well, almost everyone. I sat with my hands
clasped in my lap wishing I could shrink to the size
of a pine needle so I could hop on the beetle crawling
between my feet and make a silent getaway.

The next few minutes stretched on for hours as

Becca giggled and shrieked her way through the funny, surprising, and often-thoughtful gifts everyone kept giving her.

"It's a vegan candy cookbook," Annie said, pointing to the title that read *Vegan Candy Cookbook*.

"That looks so fun," Becca responded. "Thank you."

"Do mine next," Kirsten pleaded.

Becca unwrapped a box with a shirt that said *Got Veggies?*

"It's perfect," Becca said, holding up the shirt while beaming at her best friend.

Ben plunked a heavy package next to her wrapped in brown paper.

"You think those are presents? Get a load of what I got you!"

Becca pulled back the paper to reveal a metal bucket full of vegetables.

"They're from my mom's garden," Ben boasted.

"They look delicious," Becca's mom commented.

Ben nodded, lowering his voice.

"Just don't tell my mom. And I'm going to need the bucket back."

That got everyone giggling. I even added a tight-lipped snort; I was that moved.

Last but not least, Jackson handed her a box wrapped in shimmering red paper with a white bow taped to the top. Becca carefully removed the bow and held it up to the firelight.

"Is the bow handmade?"

Jackson gave a sheepish shrug.

"My mom's into that kind of stuff. She taught me at our last church craft night."

"It's beautiful!" Kirsten said, taking the bow from Becca.

He really was the worst. Seriously.

Becca opened the box and pulled out a stuffed bear with bright red fur and a smile that would have looked perfect on a creepy killer-clown doll. The moment she hugged it to her chest an even creepier voice spoke: "Let's cuddle."

"It's a Cuddle Bear!" Carly shrieked, running to Becca and pulling the creepy killer-clown bear from her grasp.

Becca giggled uncontrollably, watching her sister

hug the bear as if the bear were real, and actually cuddly.

"You have to understand," Becca explained to the group. "Jackson and I have to watch the show every afternoon because our sisters love the Cuddle Bears. I told him all I wanted for my birthday was a Cuddle Bear of my very own."

"And you got your wish," Jackson added.

"It's perfect," she replied, still giggling.

And then she got up, walked over, and gave him a hug. An actual hug right in front of everyone. And that's when I knew: I had been right all along. They really were going out. And I really was nothing more than the butt end of a bad joke. The sort of joke where a spindly kid gets tricked into believing he might actually be studly. But I wasn't Harley with his greasy mustache, black leather vest, and fairyland barn. There would be no happy ending to my story.

I should have known.

**54**

"Okay, is that everyone?" Becca's mom asked.

No one spoke, but more than a few eyes strayed my way. Actually, everyone's eyes strayed my way. Everyone's except Becca's. She ignored me as if my lack of a present was no big deal, which hurt most of all. I could withstand a few accusing stares, but being ignored by Becca left me feeling cold and empty—as if my insides had been slurped out.

After that, Becca's dad brought out a cake and everyone sang "Happy Birthday." I mumbled along trying not to notice Jackson standing next to Becca or the way he helped her blow out the candles after her first attempt failed.

"Dude, even your lungs are ripped," Ben joked after

Jackson's gale-force breath nearly tore the last candle out of the cake.

If only I had a wooden stake and a hammer. We'd see whose lungs were ripped then.

After eating cake off paper plates, the party turned into a lot of hugging and awkward standing around. The hugging referred to the way Becca kept thanking everyone for their thoughtful presents. The awkward standing around mostly referred to me while I watched all the hugging taking place. Not to mention watching Ben continue to joke around with Jackson. And Jackson continue to hang around Becca. And Ryan continue to avoid being anywhere near Gretchen. And Tyler—come to think of it, where was Tyler?

That question got answered a moment later when he and Annie slipped out of the woods and rejoined the group. He gave us a shrug. He hadn't kissed her, had he? They weren't even going out anymore.

"How does he do it?" Ben asked, also staring at Tyler.

"I don't know. But I'm really starting to hate that guy."

"I'm with you. He's a menace."

"A menace with pouty, irresistible lips."

"You got that right."

By this point, the sun had gone down, the fire had burned low, and goose bumps covered any skin not covered in pants or a sweatshirt. Which included my arms and legs since I hadn't thought to bring either pants or a sweatshirt.

Finally, parents began arriving and everyone lined up to give their goodbyes to the birthday girl. Mostly everyone. My parents were late as always, so I stood off to the side shivering while waving to the lucky souls who had brought presents, received hugs in return, and were now going home in warm cars.

"Want to walk down to the pier and look at the water?"

I turned to find Becca next to me. How had she gotten that close without me noticing?

"My parents will probably be here any moment."

She headed for the trail that led to the water.

"Don't worry, my parents will get us when they arrive."

Honestly, the last thing I needed was to go for a walk with someone else's girlfriend. "Sure."

Maybe just a short walk.

The trail wound down through the silhouetted trees. In the distance, we caught glimpses of the bay and the moon reflecting off the dark water.

"It's kinda creepy," Becca said.

She reached out and took my hand. An electric current prickled up my arm.

"Yeah," I squeaked.

What exactly was going on here? A whirl of confusion swirled in my brain. Would she be holding my hand if she and Jackson were really going out? Should I just ask her and get it over with? Or should I keep my mouth shut and for once in my life let a moment be a moment? In truth, I desperately wanted to ask, but my lips refused to open far enough for any words to get out. Smart lips.

We slid down a short steep slope and reached the pier. It stretched out about fifty yards into the bay held above the water by wooden pilings. Overhead, a full moon gleamed in all its nighttime glory. Murmuring waves lapped rhythmically on the rocky beach.

"C'mon," Becca said, tugging my hand.

Leaving the covering shadows of the trail, we skipped down the pier until we reached the far end. We huddled together against the cold staring out at the murky waters.

"Isn't it beautiful?" Becca asked.

I had to admit looking at the bay lit only by moonlight was pretty cool. "Yeah, it's really something."

"And it's a full moon."

"Yeah."

She turned to face me, her hand releasing mine.

"Can I ask you something?"

"I guess so."

"Did I do something?"

"What do you mean?"

Her eyes lowered.

"I mean, at the start of the summer, we were hanging out. And then we stopped."

The zombie warlord in my chest let out a moan. It

wasn't *my* fault we stopped hanging out. Was it? "Well, it's just that—I thought—I'm sorry I didn't bring a present."

Her eyes looked up, not angry, or even annoyed. Just . . . hurt.

"It's okay. It was just a dumb birthday party."

But that wasn't it at all. "No, it wasn't that. I really wanted to do something nice. I was going to—you know—like—write you a"—I strained to get the last word out—"poem."

The last word sounded like about the dumbest idea ever in the history of dumb ideas. But she didn't laugh. Not even a giggle.

"Why didn't you?"

Why didn't I? That seemed pretty obvious. "Well— because—you know—you and—Jackson."

Her eyes went wide. Really wide. I'm pretty sure I saw China on the back side of one eyeball.

"You think Jackson and I are going out?"

And that's when the zombie warlord fainted right there in my chest. THEY WEREN'T GOING OUT?

"Aren't you?"

Her face turned from shock to laughter.

"No! What made you think we were going out?"

Uh . . . what kind of idiot would assume something like that? The answer seemed clear. A total blubbering idiot. The sort of total blubbering idiot who would jump to a conclusion simply because the two of them had been hanging out together the entire summer. Wait a minute! They had been hanging out together the entire summer! "But you've been hanging out with him all summer."

She shrugged.

"Our sisters are best friends. And our parents are both making us watch our little sisters all summer. We didn't really have a choice. Don't get me a wrong, Jackson is a nice guy. But we're not going out."

The zombie warlord gave a weak whimper and tried to sit up. "Oh."

"Did you really think we were going out?"

That answer suddenly seemed pretty silly. "Well—"

She shook her head, her shoulders relaxing.

"And I thought you were mad at me."

"I could never be mad at you."

Her eyes returned to mine.

"Really?"

"Really."

A new look crossed her face. One I was more familiar with, her mischievous look.

"So what sort of poem were you writing?"

"Um—sort of an—uh—I-kinda-like-you poem."

"Really?"

The zombie warlord got back up and returned to his usual pastime hammering on my ribs. "But I never finished it."

Her mischievous eyes glowed brighter.

"Why don't you finish it now?"

Seriously? Here? Right in front of her? If the zombie warlord had been hammering before he was pounding for all he was worth now. And then somehow the words came to me in a rush. Simple, sweet, and from the heart.

"Roses are red, and violets are blue," I started. And now for the big finish. "I'm not a dork, when I'm with you."

Okay, maybe not a poetic masterpiece, but it did get

a giggle. And not just from me. She reached out and took my hands.

"Less of a dork," she corrected, leaning in.

And then before the universe could stop it from happening, our lips touched. Like really touched. I literally felt my head contract and then explode like in the zombie bride scene in *Death Intruders*. Exactly like Ben said it would. And it was the most awesome exploding-head death ever.

"C'mon, Becca, it's time to go!"

Our lips parted. I looked down to find Carly pulling on Becca's arm.

"C'mon, Mom and Dad are waiting!"

Sure enough, Becca's parents were standing at the end of the pier. Next to my parents. Of course. How else could my first kiss end?

"I guess it's time to head back," Becca said, sounding disappointed.

"Ug, gerrh," I babbled like an infant.

On the way home, I found my arms still covered in goose bumps, but not from the cold. Something life-changing had happened on the pier. Something mysterious that would probably take a lifetime to unravel. Or to at least wonder if it would ever happen again.

After we got home, my father stopped by my room to say good night.

"So, how you doin'?"

What sort of question was that? "Good."

"Good? Is that all?"

To be honest, I was doing slightly better than good. Something more along the lines of UNBELIEVABLY FANTASTIC! But I wasn't about to let that on. "Yeah. Good."

He shook his head and headed for the hall.

"Just one thing," he said, pulling the door closed behind him. "At some point you're gonna want to wipe that silly grin off your face."

He gave me a parting wink.

"But take your time. And hold on to the memory. You don't want to let go of that one."

That was for darn sure.

I found my grandmother's store buzzing with activity the next morning. An impromptu party seemed to be taking place, complete with a buffet of scrambled eggs, bacon, and a pile of donuts covered in sprinkles.

"Betty at the Sunshine Café brought all this over," Elsa announced. "She wanted to do something nice for us the day after the show."

My grandmother handed me a paper plate.

"Help yourself," she said. "You deserve something special after everything you did to make the show a success."

I piled a mound of bacon on the plate along with a couple donuts. I guess I did pretty much single-handedly save the show. My hand slipped, and half my bacon slid off onto the floor. Okay, maybe *single-handedly* was a bit of an overstatement.

"Seemed like everyone had a good time," I suggested.

"Seemed like?" Diane asked.

She took a slurp from her coffee mug.

"All I keep hearing is how much people loved the show!"

Elsa put an arm around Diane and squeezed. "What was not to love? We had the very best models on the very best stage in the very best venue ever!"

Aiko wrapped an arm around Diane from the other side.

"Will the show use local models again?" she asked.

"Absolutely," my grandmother answered. "After watching this year's show, we've decided from now on only local talent will be used. And Stefan is on board to be an official sponsor next year."

Harley stopped in, followed by Kirsten, Becca, and Ben.

"Looks like we got here just in time," Harley said, giving Elsa a hug and me a high five.

Ben also gave me a high five while his other hand stole the remaining bacon off my plate.

"Quite the party happening here," he said, munching down my bacon.

"Sounds like we left Becca's party a little early last night," Kirsten added, giving me an all-too-knowing smile.

Becca elbowed Kirsten's side.

"Ignore her," Becca said, her cheeks flushing. "She's just being annoying."

Ben froze, a piece of bacon half jammed into his gaping mouth.

"Did I miss something?"

Did he ever. "Nope."

He tilted his head back and eyed me and Becca. I prayed my cheeks weren't burning as hot as hers. At last, he let out a breath and bit down on the bacon.

Whew. That had been close.

A moment later, he pulled me aside.

"You dog!"

What?

"You and Becca kissed, didn't you?"

"What? No—never—well—you know—maybe."

"I knew it. I knew it was gonna happen."

No, he didn't. Except I guess he *had* called it from the start.

"You the man!"

True, my self-esteem had gotten a pretty good boost in the last couple days. But I wasn't the only one. I looked around at Elsa and Harley chatting together. And Diane and my grandmother walking to the back of the store with their arms entwined. When you thought about it, maybe girls weren't really so different from guys. And maybe adults weren't so different from kids. Everyone has fears. And insecurities.

A piece of bacon and half a donut jammed into my gut.

"Dude, cram the bacon and donut in your mouth at the same time," Ben demanded. "It's the best!"

And occasionally a moment when everything fits together perfectly. Like a salty mouthful of bacon mixed with the sugary goodness of a donut. Or when your girlfriend shakes her head in disgust at you but her lips are smiling.

And somehow you know, at least for a while, that everything is going to be all right.